SHE QUIVERED WITH LONGING

as his hands caressed her with sure possession. He reached out to pull her against him with such force that it took her breath away. At first, his mouth was gentle on hers, softly searching until he felt her response. Then the kiss hardened with urgency and desire surfacing in a storm that made Carrie's body melt against his hard masculine strength. She clung to him then as though she would never let him go again. . . .

Other SIGNET Books by Glenna Finley

STORM
OF DESIRE

by
Glenna Finley

A SIGNET BOOK
NEW AMERICAN LIBRARY
TIMES MIRROR

NAL BOOKS ARE ALSO AVAILABLE AT DISCOUNTS
IN BULK QUANTITY FOR INDUSTRIAL OR
SALES-PROMOTIONAL USE. FOR DETAILS, WRITE TO
PREMIUM MARKETING DIVISION, NEW AMERICAN LIBRARY, INC.,
1301 AVENUE OF THE AMERICAS, NEW YORK, NEW YORK 10019.

COPYRIGHT © 1977 BY GLENNA FINLEY

SIGNET TRADEMARK REG. U.S. PAT. OFF. AND FOREIGN COUNTRIES
REGISTERED TRADEMARK—MARCA REGISTRADA
HECHO EN CHICAGO, U.S.A.

SIGNET, SIGNET CLASSICS, MENTOR, PLUME AND MERIDIAN BOOKS
are published by The New American Library, Inc.,
1301 Avenue of the Americas, New York, New York 10019

FIRST SIGNET PRINTING, FEBRUARY, 1977

1 2 3 4 5 6 7 8 9

PRINTED IN THE UNITED STATES OF AMERICA

"Love—all a wonder and a wild desire."

—BROWNING

Chapter One

It was cold on Hilton Head Island that morning in early December.

Carrie Shaw heard the cabbage-palm fronds rustle protestingly as she started down the path to the South Island marina and felt an instant's commiseration. The word "South" in South Carolina ought to mean something. Like warm, caressing breezes instead of a biting wind off the Atlantic which had the scarlet ensign atop the marina snapping on its aluminum pole. It even ruffled the waters out in mid-channel, where two sturdy shrimp trawlers steamed leisurely toward the ocean, ready to start sweeping the offshore currents with their fine nets.

All things down south seemed to move at that unhurried pace in the off-season, Carrie thought irritably, wishing she had pockets in her slacks so she could warm her cold fingers. If she'd known things were this deserted, she would have had second thoughts about driving a balky car down to watch the sunrise over the water. Especially after she'd tried to start the motor a little later and the only result was a moan from the car's innards. Now it looked as if she were going to trade her insomnia for a case of double pneumonia unless she could find someone to diagnose her car's trouble.

She stared hopefully at the quiet length of dock ahead of her, where the pleasure boats bobbed peacefully, the sailboats shrouded in their canvas wrappings and the power boats locked and secure. It was a pretty picture, but not one of her choosing just then. As she pulled to a stop and blew on her cold knuckles, she came to the reluctant conclusion that this part of the marina was as deserted as the parking lot.

She had half-turned to retrace her footsteps when a slight disturbance in the water made her swing around and stare frowning at the gleaming Bayliner cruiser in the berth just beyond a thirty-five-foot sailboat. Its decks were as vacant and undisturbed as its neighbors', but the bow of the boat was rocking considerably more—making it appear as if someone had just gone aboard.

Carrie stood undecided, wondering if it justified a closer inspection on her part. Then she moved slowly toward it, deciding to satisfy her curiosity before she gradually became an icy addition to the deck.

She moved past the deserted sailboat and pulled up cautiously alongside the cruiser. The motion of the boat was subsiding, but it still moved more than its snug mooring warranted. Carrie stood on tiptoe and surveyed the immaculate afterdeck, noticing suddenly that the sliding glass door leading into the cruiser's cabin wasn't completely closed. Even then she would have given up the idea of exploring further if she hadn't suddenly sighted a trail of water glistening on the nonskid surface of the deck. Someone *had* come aboard, and recently, too, she decided triumphantly.

Impulsively Carrie stepped over the rail onto the cruiser's stern, giving silent thanks for her slacks and rubber-soled shoes. The rest of her appearance could have stood some improving, she decided, even for an impromptu boarding party. The wind had played havoc with her taffy-colored hair, and her neat chignon was a thing of the past. Probably her lipstick had disappeared about the same time. Her soft-curved mouth straightened into a determined line. After all, she told herself, this was hardly a social call. The owner of the cruiser wouldn't notice such trivialities.

As she peeked past the glass door into the luxurious cabin, an uneasy expression crossed her face. There wasn't a sign of anyone in the compact and comfortable surroundings; she must have been imagining things, after all.

The motion of the craft made a folding door at the bow of the cabin slide gently back on its hardware, and Carrie let out a breath of relief. The owner had simply sought the privacy of the forward cabin, still hidden from view. She reached up to knock on the glass panel and then discarded

3

the thought. Instead she pushed it aside and called hesitantly.

"Excuse me ... could I speak to you for a minute, please? I need your help. ..."

A silence as thick as the concrete pier followed her words. When the seconds passed and there was still no response, Carrie's trim figure stiffened in apprehension. For the first time, she because aware of the total isolation of the dock and the fact that no one in the world knew where she was. She had just started to make a strategic and hasty retreat when the door to the forward cabin was suddenly shoved aside and a tall masculine figure emerged, wearing a pair of denim shorts as his only covering. That they'd been hastily donned was obvious from the way he glared at her. There was an instant's pause; then he strode through the main cabin toward her and came to a halt at the glass door.

Even as she opened her lips to frame her explanation, he reached down and caught her wrist.

"What in the hell are you playing at?" he demanded in deep, angry tones. "How did you know I was here?"

Carrie's polite greeting stopped in her throat. Her mouth dropped open, and her delicate brows shot up. Instinctively she yanked at her wrist with all the effect of a housefly battering against armor plate. "What do you think you're doing?" she got out finally. Her voice sounded thin to her own ears, and she tried to steady it. "If you don't let go of me this minute, I'll scream my head off."

His grip didn't loosen one iota. "Go ahead. You're not getting off the hook until I learn who sent you." His dark eyes narrowed unpleasantly as they raked her length. "Whoever it was should have told you that I object to uninvited guests. Even pretty little girls with measurements like yours."

His last remark acted like a fuse to Carrie's temper which until then had lain dormant. "Listen, you overage Casanova," she snarled back at him in a tone that was as cold as the December wind then gusting over the water, "nobody sent me. If you think they did, you're obviously suffering from delusions or palpitations or something. Maybe your early-morning dip was too much for your nervous system." She nodded toward the glistening wet suit that he'd left on the cabin floor when he emerged.

Her captor half-turned to follow her glance, and then a muscle tightened in his jaw as his head swung back. "You don't miss a thing, do you?"

Carrie gave another futile yank against his grip even as she said, "You're not making a bit of sense. I came down here trying to see if I could get somebody to help me with my car. Obviously I knocked on the wrong door," she went on scathingly as she saw his brows draw together. "Why don't you just forget the whole thing? I'll leave, and you can go on your merry way. So if you'll kindly remove your hand from my wrist..."

For a moment she thought she'd won as his grip lessened while he continued to stare down at her from his six-foot height. "Your story sounds almost flaky enough to be true," he said finally. "Nobody in his right mind would use car trouble for an alibi these days. I suppose you drove down to look at the sunrise . . ."

Her cheeks flushed at his mocking tone. "As a matter of fact, I did. But after this, I certainly won't try it again." She attempted to free her hand as he hesitated, obviously weighing her story.

She would have been successful and back on the dock if there hadn't been a strident hail just then from a man on the porch of the marina.

"Hey, you . . . down there!"

With one accord, Carrie and her captor turned, and she gasped with pain as she felt the grasp on her wrist harden when he apparently recognized the caller.

"Damn it to hell!" he swore softly. "*Now* see what you've done!"

"What I've done? You're out of your mind!"

"Mark . . . is that you?" There was a moment of arrested movement, and then the man at the marina took a flight of steps two at a time as he started down the dock toward them. "Hold it right there!" he called out.

The man holding Carrie at the stern of the cruiser shot a calculating glance toward the advancing figure. Then he dropped his other arm around her shoulders to pull her close, and bending down, kissed her heartily.

The one-sided embrace lasted only a moment, and Carrie was hustled back into the cabin of the cruiser before she could even start to protest. Her captor hesitated just for an instant by the folding door that masked the forward cabin, and then, instead, opened a wooden door next to it and shoved Carrie into the tiny room beyond. "Don't say a word," he warned her brusquely, "not if you want to get out in one piece." Even as he spoke, he was closing the door and turning the key in the lock outside. A minute later she heard the hum of a motor, and then a transistor radio nearby blared forth with a program of rock music.

Instinctively she started to pound on the door. Then she dropped her arm as she realized that she'd been unceremoniously thrust into the tiny bathroom and shower cubicle of the cruiser. There was a molded fiberglass shower and a compact lavatory which took up one side of the room, while behind her, the only hidden recess was at eye level. She pushed eagerly at the sliding door and found a tiny medicine cabinet rather than the porthole or vent she'd hoped to reveal.

Her jailer had picked his spot well, she decided irritably. There was no chance to escape, and no hope of shouting over a radio turned to full volume. As for a weapon ... Her glance swung around the room again, and she sagged dispiritedly against the wall at the end of her reconnaissance. She had her choice of a comb, a battery razor, or a tube of toothpaste and a green-handled toothbrush. Not even a nail file to loosen screws. Even if there were screws. Which there weren't. "Damn!" Carrie said angrily, and folded her arms over her

7

chest. The latter movement wasn't merely a gesture of defiance; one of the things missing in the bathroom was a heater. She shivered as she edged over to the door and put her ear against it. With any luck, that creature who hailed them would insist on searching the cruiser. If she could only hear something besides that miserable music . . .

It was as well for her peace of mind that Carrie couldn't overhear the exchange taking place just then on the afterdeck.

The man who had run down the dock was still breathing heavily as he stood on the side of the boat saying disgustedly to Carrie's captor, "Next time you start playing games, Mark, for god's sake, clue me in. I thought you were gone for the weekend and somebody was ransacking the cruiser."

"Sorry, Rudy," Mark said, reaching in a locker and dragging out a corduroy robe. "You can understand why I didn't send out announcements."

"The girl?" Rudy shoved his hands in the pockets of a well-tailored pair of faded denims. He looked annoyed but resigned as he peered into the cabin. "What did you do with her?"

"She's shy." Mark tightened the belt on his robe. "Not accustomed to company."

"I'll bet." There was a strong measure of sarcasm in the other's tone. "From what I saw, I admire your taste—I'd enjoy meeting her."

"Sorry. I'm not fool enough to invite competition. You have enough listings in your black book without adding any of my . . . friends." He leaned back against the glass door and casually surveyed the other's wiry frame. Rudy Forza was a man in his late twenties—a few years younger than Mark— with black hair worn collar-length, slumbrous dark eyes, and a profile that would have been envied by a Roman emperor.

Rudy stared back, his relaxed bearing showing complete confidence under the other's regard. He even seemed amused by Mark's words. "Better in my black book than other places," he told him. "If Angela hears about this interlude, there'll be hell for you to pay." As Mark's eyebrows arched, he realized he'd gone too far. "Sorry, I didn't mean to sound like a big brother, but you haven't seen Angela when she's in a temper. The last hurricane was tame by comparison."

"Naturally, I'd hate to cause your sister any unhappiness . . ." There was subtle warning in Mark's smooth deep tone, "but the last I heard, we were both free, white, and all the rest. So maybe we'd both better forget about this conversation. Make yourself useful and cast off for me, will you?"

Rudy grinned. "I wasn't aware that I was leaving. So you're not going to introduce me to your . . . guest?"

"I always said that you were a very perceptive man."

"Okay." Forza seemed to realize that there was no point in arguing further, and he stepped across to the dock. "I haven't seen a thing. Are you still having dinner with Angela and me tomorrow night?"

"If the invitation still holds." Mark sounded as if he didn't care either way.

Rudy sighed as he leaned over to release the cruiser's bow line. "It still holds. And if you want to bring along a friend ..."

"If we're both talking about the same lady, don't count on it. Her talents run in a different direction than dinner-table conversation." With that, Mark nodded tersely, closed the glass panel, and went forward to slide onto the pilot's seat in mid-cabin.

Despite his casual movement, he knew to the instant when Rudy tossed the stern line on deck and cut the blower lever as soon as the cruiser was free. An instant later, he'd switched on the craft's powerful engines, revved them carefully, and was easing away from the dock with the skill of long practice.

As soon as the motion of the cruiser became apparent, he heard a muffled pounding on the lavatory door. He waited until the boat was safely out in mid-channel heading across the deserted waters of the sound before he leaned over and shut off the radio. An instant later, he cut the engines to idling speed and went down to turn the key in the lock.

"It's okay," he said on confronting Carrie's furious figure. "You can come out now." Without waiting to see her reaction, he moved back onto the pilot's bench and adjusted the throttles to cruising speed.

"You have one hell of a nerve!" Carrie burst out. She looked around in bewilderment and then came up the step to the center of the cabin. "You can't *do* this, I tell you! Where do you think you're taking me?"

He winced. "Do you have to make it sound like a white-slave expedition? Believe me, lady, you'll be on your way just as soon as I can think of a safe place to put you ashore. It can't be too soon for me."

She was looking desperately around the cabin for some kind of weapon to reinforce her position when his words penetrated. Turning, she stared at him in amazement. "If you wanted to get rid of me, why didn't you just let me go ashore back there?"

"Because I couldn't trust you to keep your pretty little trap shut," he said, sounding sick and tired of the entire discussion. "Since I'd gone to a lot of trouble to convince Rudy that we'd just spent a night of sinful bliss, I didn't want the effect spoiled."

"You did what?" Her voice rose, horrified.

"You heard me. After that, I could hardly dump you ashore at his feet and ask if he'd check out the engine on your goddamned car.

"You don't have to get nasty about it." She rubbed her forehead as if she couldn't believe what was happening. "I'm the one who's being kidnapped, for heaven's sake." As he simply snorted, she clenched her fists in sudden temper. "Well, I am. How dare you shut me in that horrible room and threaten me! I imagined all sorts of things. Any woman would when a naked man attacks her."

"I was *not* naked, and I did *not* attack you."

"Well, you kissed me . . ."

"There *is* a difference," he pointed out dryly. "That was just embroidery for your cover story. Anyway, I didn't invite you aboard. That was your idea."

Carrie examined her fingernails carefully to hide the triumph that was beginning to surge through her. The man didn't sound like the fiend she'd first thought him; nor did he look as if he were suffering any mental or sexual aberrations. He was more than ordinarily good-looking—a tall, well-proportioned man with dark hair and eyes, whose outstanding characteristic just then was sheer annoyance. If the newspapers were to be believed, villains didn't come in that mold; seldom did they show such eagerness to dispense with female company and be on their way . . . alone.

Not that she approved of his actions, she told herself hastily, but at least she could hear him out. So far, it was more interesting than sitting on a deserted beach communing with nature on a morning more geared for staying in bed. The thought of cozy blankets made her conscious of another complaint.

"I'm cold," she said succinctly. "It was utterly

freezing in that bathroom. I won't forget to tell the authorities about that, either."

"Far be it from me to spoil your story, but the heater's right under there," he said, jerking a thumb toward the bottom of the couch. "Turn up the thermostat. I could do with some warm air myself."

"I'm not surprised," she said as she surveyed him. "Don't you believe in clothes? You're not doing your cause any good by running around like that, you know."

"Oh, I *do* know," he replied with elaborate sarcasm. "So far, I've subjected you to the frozen elements, terrified you with my naked form, and made unwelcome advances. Anything else?"

She thought it over carefully. "You can add slow starvation. I haven't had any breakfast."

"I thought you were too upset to eat."

She went over to stand by the heater. "I'll force myself. After all, I have to keep up my strength so I can escape."

"That won't be necessary. I'm beginning to have second thoughts."

"You mean like cooking breakfast for us?" She sat down on the attractive upholstered bench, keeping her ankles in front of the heater's warm air. "That might help you in court. I could say that you repented when faced with the realization of your crime."

He gave her a sardonic look. "That wasn't what I had in mind. If you're not careful, I'll check

13

you out on long-distance swimming. I've had about enough of this chitchat."

Carrie's newfound triumph took a sudden retreat, and her grayish-blue eyes grew large with fright.

"Oh, hell!" Mark squirmed uncomfortably on his bench. "I'm not about to toss you overboard. Not if you behave yourself," he added, altering his tone as he heard her make a noise of satisfaction. "Just fix some coffee, will you?"

"*I'm* the prisoner," she began, and then saw his jaw line harden. "Oh, all right." She got to her feet. "But it certainly is a strange way of doing things."

"I wish you'd make up your mind. One minute you're ready for a nervous breakdown, and the next thing, you're complaining because we're not awash with corpses. Can't you be satisfied with a night of clandestine love? I'm talking about *last* night," he added hurriedly as she turned toward him with the percolator in her hand. "The one I told Rudy about."

"Oh, that."

She didn't sound altogether displeased, and he frowned at her.

"It was a ridiculous thing to say," she went on hastily.

"What would you have suggested in the circumstances? Rudy would have laughed his head off if I'd told him your version."

"Not necessarily. Especially not if I confirmed it." She gave him a quizzical look. "This story of yours ... you couldn't have been trying for a reason to explain *your* presence, could you?"

"Why should I need an alibi? It's my boat."

She wrinkled her nose and nodded slowly. "I suppose you're right. Well, none of it makes sense to me, but it really doesn't matter."

"Why is that?"

"I don't live down here." She was searching in the cupboard under the stove. "Where do you keep the coffee?"

"Lower shelf on the right-hand side," he replied automatically. Then he added, "Wait a minute—come here and take the controls while I get some clothes on. I'll make the coffee afterward."

Carrie stood where she was, still clutching the coffeepot. "I don't think you know what you're asking. Other than a ten-day cruise I took to the Caribbean once, my maritime experience is strictly nil."

"Don't worry—at this rate, you can't do any harm. Just sit here and keep your eyes peeled for deadheads in the water. Floating logs or debris ... that kind of thing," he added impatiently when she stared at him.

"If you're sure ..."

He took the coffeepot from her grasp and gestured toward the pilot's bench. "Of course I am. For pete's sake, it's not a lifetime career."

"I know that." She slid gingerly along the seat. "It just doesn't make sense."

"What doesn't make sense?"

"Letting me take over the controls."

A fleeting grin passed over his tired face. "You mean since you're being abducted? Remember that when you report to the authorities. It may shorten my sentence."

She watched him disappear in the forward cabin and called after him, "Don't think I won't. This may be funny to you, but it's still kidnapping pure and simple. . . ." Her words trailed off as the folding door closed behind him. She grimaced in annoyance and shifted her gaze to methodically check the water around them.

Inwardly her thoughts were considerably more erratic—occupied wholly by the stranger getting dressed a few feet away. Sometime soon, Carrie thought, she'd have to ask his name.

"How are things going up there?" His stern voice made her sit up straighter.

"Er . . . fine." She glanced around and said again, more confidently, "Everything's fine."

There was the sound of the door being pushed aside, and he appeared, wearing jeans and an Irish turtleneck sweater that he was still pulling over his hips. He gave a quick look at the water around them and let his glance flick over her. "I thought you might be trying to radio the Coast Guard for help."

"I didn't even think about it." She returned his glance coolly. "Are you going to make the coffee now?"

"That comes right after I put on some shoes and socks." He gestured toward a small mainland settlement which was just visible on the starboard side. "I thought we'd tie up at a shrimp-boat dock down there while we have breakfast. Unless you'd rather skip eating. . . ."

"What do you mean?" She was watching him drag a pair of canvas shoes out of a storage locker and sit down on the steps by the small galley to put them on.

"Well, if you're in a hurry to get back to the island, I could hire one of the locals to take you there."

"A friend of yours?" Her tone was thick with suspicion.

"My god, no!" He knotted his shoelace with such emphasis that it was a wonder it didn't come apart in his hands. "If you'd rather, I'll let you phone for a nice neutral taxicab. How does that sound?"

"Better," she admitted.

"Okay, then. Move over, and I'll handle the controls." He jerked his thumb toward the luxurious cabin behind them. "Sit down and make yourself comfortable. This shouldn't take long."

Carrie did as he asked, letting him slide onto the bench before he reached over and grasped the throttles. Immediately the cruiser's speed doubled, and she had to hang on as the bow cut into the offshore swells.

"Better sit down," he cautioned.

She chose to sit on the step where he'd changed his shoes, so that she could watch his profile as he concentrated on the wooden dock a half-mile away. It wasn't a bad profile, she decided, trying to be impartial. As a matter of fact, it was darned good. Rugged and determined, but with lines at the corners of his mouth which showed that sometimes he must smile. Not that he'd done much of it since she'd come aboard.

Her quiet survey must have made itself felt, because he half-turned his head to intercept her glance. "What's going on in that mind of yours now?" he wanted to know.

She leaned against the galley partition. "That it might be nice to know your name." As he hesitated, she went on sweetly, "When I go to the police—it's so much easier to sign an official complaint." She had the satisfaction of seeing his brows meet in a forbidding line. "My name is Carrie Shaw—or Catherine, if you want to be formal."

His expression softened at her overture. "How do you do, Miss Catherine Shaw," he said, revealing that he was no stranger to feminine wiles. "I'm Mark Ralston." Her expression must have surprised him. "What's the matter? Did you expect me to say Joe Smith?"

She nodded. "I guess I did. Mark Ralston from where?"

"Savannah now. Philadelphia before that."

"I thought you sounded more like the Main Line than Mason-Dixon."

"I could say the same thing about you," he pointed out, considering.

"You're right." She traced her finger absently along the crease on her slacks. "Indianapolis now.

But Savannah originally. Even Hilton Head a few years later."

"You mean you have friends around here?" Obviously her announcement had disconcerted him.

"Why, yes." She stood up and stretched before peering through the glass of the cabin window. "You did invite me for breakfast, didn't you?" Her tone was slightly curious.

"But I thought you couldn't wait to get ..." He caught himself and changed tactics. "Whatever you say. I should warn you that I'm not a very good cook. You'd fare better ashore."

The last vestige of fear left Carrie at his obvious desire to speed her on her way. But along with the relief came a distinctly annoyed feeling. She wasn't in the habit of having any man try to get rid of her. Around the age of eighteen, she had learned to appreciate the cadence of an admiring wolf whistle from the male sex, and the ensuing five years had done nothing to change her attitude. But apparently something was missing in the magic formula as far as this stranger was concerned.

Her reasoning wasn't far wrong. Mark Ralston was far too busy and preoccupied to do any girl-watching just then. He had decided that the best thing was to send Catherine Something-or-other on her way without delay. He glanced at her profile absently, his mind on other things.

"If you'll excuse me," the object of his scrutiny told him, "I'll go and comb my hair. Do you mind if I leave the door *un*locked this time?"

He flushed slightly. "Be my guest."

"Thanks." She smiled on him. "I intend to."

His eyebrows drew together again, and he scowled at her retreating figure until she closed the door. Then he muttered, "Damnation!" and transferred his gaze back to the approaching dock. He'd spent enough time on boats so that he could make all the necessary moves automatically, and Carrie would have been cheered to know that she was very much in his thoughts as he slowed the engines and prepared to come alongside the deserted jetty.

Their relationship had undergone a distinct change in the last few minutes, and Mark wasn't happy with the new state of affairs. While he hadn't wanted to frighten her, he wasn't prepared to stand around half the morning answering silly questions, either. He hadn't misread her final message; thirty years' experience told him that madame had him squarely where she wanted him and wasn't about to let him off the hook. Not until he came up with some answers. He rubbed his chin thoughtfully. Of course, he could make a pass at her. That might speed her on her way. Or speed him straight to the pokey, he decided, after remembering that last look of hers.

Besides, she knew people around. Just his luck to tangle with a returning native. Why couldn't he have managed to find an honest-to-god tourist! And why couldn't this woman have stayed in bed where she belonged instead of watching the sunrise and lousing up his life. "Women!" he muttered. "They're the very devil!"

Carrie emerged to catch his last words. "I beg your pardon."

He cut the engines as the dock appeared alongside. "Just stay out of the way," he grated.

Carrie's eyes widened as she saw the speed with which he made fast the stern line and then repeated the process at the bow before the cruiser could drift perceptibly. Afterward he methodically checked the fenders and coiled some spare line. Each movement he made was unhurried and precise, almost as if he were deliberately avoiding her. She caught a glimpse of her reflection in a tiny mirrored panel and wrinkled her nose. "So much for new lipstick," she told herself. "I needn't have bothered."

When Mark came back into the cabin, she kept carefully out of his way as he went over to remove the key from the control panel.

"We seem to be the only people around," she said, trying to sound casual.

"Sometimes a shrimp boat will tie up here to make repairs, but there's not much else to attract them." He jerked his head toward a dirt track that led away from the end of the wharf. "There's a tavern and grocery down there through the trees. A telephone, too," he added significantly.

She didn't answer immediately, busily noting the thick stand of live oaks and palms along the shore. It was typical Carolina low-country scenery, with a peaceful air that belonged more to turn-of-the-century life than present-day bustle. "Hardly a thriving center of commerce," she murmured finally.

"Some of the offshore islands are almost Civil War vintage in their way of life," he commented. "A little different from the pace on Hilton Head. Now, if your car engine had conked out here, you would have been in trouble."

"Strange you'd say that." Her tone was cool. "After what's happened I thought I'd picked the worst possible place."

He winced and reached up to trace an X in the air. "Score one for you, Miss ... er ... Catherine ..." His forehead wrinkled as he obviously tried to recall her name.

"Shaw," she snapped. "Carrie Shaw."

If he noted her annoyance, he didn't let on. "I'd better make that coffee." He rubbed a hand over the back of his neck wearily. "Otherwise I'll fall asleep standing up."

She watched him start spooning coffee into the pot before putting it atop the burner on the stainless-steel range. Once that was done, he reached in the under-counter refrigerator and brought out a carton of eggs. "Soft-boiled okay with you?" he wanted to know, scarcely bothering to look over his shoulder.

"I guess so. ..."

That time, her tone got through to him. He turned to look at her as he filled a saucepan half-full of water. "Sorry there's not more choice. I don't do much cooking aboard." As she still stood uncertainly by the control panel, he reached over to give her a plastic container full of cutlery. "You can set the table if you want to save time. The butter's down here in the refrigerator, and the dishes are behind that sliding panel right beside you. I'll toast some bread in the oven at the last minute."

As she started to lay out two places on the Formica dinette table at one side of the cabin, he added, "There are some place mats around, but it's hardly worthwhile hunting for them. If you'd been a prisoner in the old days, you'd have to make do with hardtack—or maybe a slab of salt pork."

She shuddered visibly. "Next you'll be telling me that you're related to Captain Bligh." She put down the last spoon and handed back the cutlery tray. "Will that coffee be long?"

"Not very." His eyes narrowed. "Why?"

"I'll go out on the stern and get some fresh air. You weren't the only one up at the crack of dawn." She went over to slide the glass door aside. "Let me know if you need any help."

"Oh, I will." He was surveying her thoughtfully. "Sure you're not planning to duck out on me?"

"Of course not. I *told* you—"

"I know ... I know. I just wanted to take your eggs out, if that was what you had in mind."

Her lips tightened. "I'll be back." As he chuckled, she closed the glass door behind her with more force than necessary and moved out onto the aft cockpit.

There was enough motion to make her reach hurriedly for the chrome rail so that she could keep her balance. Since she'd come aboard, the brisk breeze she'd felt on the wharf at Hilton Head had become a determined December wind that felt as if it were off Arctic ice fields instead of Atlantic waters, and she shivered violently inside her nylon windbreaker. But even as she huddled beneath its covering, she felt better. For some reason, it took the fresh salt tang of the cold air to get her mind in proper working order. Fresh air and food, she told herself firmly. Then she'd be able to cope.

She took a quick look over her shoulder at the man in the galley who made it necessary for her to think straight. While it was obvious that he wasn't charmed to have her aboard, it was equally obvious to Carrie that he had some more explaining to do.

First she'd find out who this Rudy at the marina was; then she'd try to find out more of Mark's reasons for stuffing her out of sight like a bundle of dirty laundry. She was only dimly conscious of his opening the glass door behind her and saying, "Breakfast's ready. I'll put the toast in if you'll butter it."

"All right." Carrie swallowed and looked fixedly over the stern, trying to avoid the faint line of the horizon.

"What's so fascinating out there?" he asked. Then, without waiting, "My god, the temperature feels more like Maine than Carolina this morning...." His glance followed hers casually before he leaned forward to concentrate on the outlines of a pleasure boat slowly cruising the main channel. "How long has that been there?" he asked tersely.

"How long has what been there?"

"That boat, of course. Right in front of you." He turned to her, suspicion darkening his expression. "What kind of a game are you playing, Miss Shaw?"

Carrie swallowed again and hung on to the rail so hard that her fingers were white with the effort. "I'm not playing anything," she got out faintly. She tried to smile, but it was a weak grimace that brought him to her side in an instant. "Or not the kind of a game you think. I can't help it if my stomach's playing leapfrog all over the place."

"Here . . . let me help you. . . ."

He tried to put an arm around her for support, but she shook him off with surprising force. "Go away," she managed to say. "Just go away and leave me alone. But don't go too far—because afterward"—her tone was muffled as she bent over the rail—"afterward, I know damned well that I'm going to kill you for getting me into this . . . if I have the strength."

Chapter Two

An unholy mess was the most charitable way of describing what happened during the next few minutes.

Later, Carrie was to recall the details of being violently ill and clinging to the rail as if she were on a channel steamer rather than a vessel moored to a piece of the South Carolina real estate. But however solid the wharf might be, the deck of the cruiser was rivaling the bumps and grinds of a veteran Minsky headliner as the wind increased.

Eventually she felt a strong arm around her shoulders, and she was led inside the cabin. Then her face and hands were washed gently with warm water while Mark made soothing noises about the worst being over. Carrie was afraid to respond or even open her eyes; she knew by then that a glance of billowing curtains or swinging lamp chains would send her flying back to the rail.

She felt Mark's weight on the bench beside her and heard his voice saying insistently, "Here ... swallow this pill—you'll feel better in no time. Just a sip of water—I'll hold it for you."

Carrie did open her eyes at that, out of dull curiosity rather than protest. Protesting was too much trouble, and even the prospect of white slavery, so long as it was on land, had much to commend it over her current existence. She felt bound, however, to make one last stab at convention.

"Just help me ashore," she mumbled, not opening her lips far enough that he could pop the pill in. "I'll be all right then. Don't need to take anything."

"Carrie, you can't lie out there on the dock in the rain," he said firmly.

She wanted to ask when it had started raining, but that was too much trouble, too. Her stomach said so.

"Take the pill, Carrie. You'll be shipshape in no time."

Carrie shuddered at his choice of words but opened her lips and then obediently took a sip of water to wash the pill down. Once that was over, she lay back, feeling as if she'd run the marathon in the Olympics.

"You can't stay here on this bench—you'll break in half," Mark was saying from somewhere above her.

If she'd been normal, she could have told him that any division would have been welcome at that moment, and she knew very well which part of her anatomy she'd stick with. Even that swallow of water had been a mistake.

"Carrie . . . are you listening to me?"

Carrie wasn't. She kept her jaw clamped tight

27

and indulged in thoughts about the sunrise she'd seen a lifetime ago. It was a very solid sunrise for an appetizer to the day. But if she'd known about the entrée to follow . . .

Her imagination soared on that word, and she moaned as her stomach lurched.

She felt Mark's arm again. This time he was pulling her firmly to her feet. "Come on, woman."

His voice was rough, but his fingers were gentle as he cradled her head against him. "One step down . . . that's it. You can rest in here and let that pill do its work. Afterward you'll feel like a new model."

Carrie wanted to say that a new model wasn't necessary; she would have settled gladly for a shadow of her former self. Or at least enough energy so that her knees would go back to their old job of keeping her upright. As it was, she was being almost carried somewhere. . . .

While she was still thinking that over, Mark let her sag onto a soft mattress, and she opened her eyes again, this time to see a white ceiling a few feet above her head. Blissfully, there was nothing to mar its expanse, and she turned back in satisfaction. A moment later she felt a pillow being tucked under her head, and her eyelids went down even as her shoes were being slipped off. Her last thought was that the couch of sin was certainly comfortable.

A considerable time must have elapsed before she awakened. It was a gradual process; she moved restlessly and opened her eyes to stare up at a vaguely familiar ceiling. Then, as the schedule of events sorted themselves out in her mind, she pushed up on an elbow and stared about her wildly.

One glance at the tidy forward cabin was enough to confirm that it hadn't figured as the site for any orgy or assorted debaucheries. From her limited knowledge, orgies would leave more evidence than an unwrinkled bedspread and a victim who had shed only her shoes.

Not only that, a blanket had been draped over her like a snug cocoon in the interval. Her gaze wandered more slowly around the cabin, aware that the cruiser's violent motion had subsided to a gentle surge that was actually pleasing to her innards. The storm must have blown over quickly, she decided, and then tried to focus on the dial of her watch to confirm it.

It was too shadowed in the cabin for her to see the dial, so she snapped on a light built in the sloping cabin wall. The sudden brightness made her grimace as she looked at the watch, before her frown changed to incredulity.

Five o'clock ... she'd been asleep most of the day! As she slithered across the mattress to stand on the floor, her hand came into contact with a strange body, and she let out a surprised yelp.

Mark shoved aside the door an instant later, in time to find her staring at a small stuffed lion made of caramel suede, which was lying on the blanket.

"You don't have to worry," he said laconically. "He's already eaten."

Carrie looked up at him apologetically, even as she ran her hand gently over the piece of sheepskin that formed the lion's mane. "I didn't know ..." she began. "That is, I couldn't see him, and I thought ..."

"I can imagine what you thought." Mark deposited the stuffed figure on a teak shelf by the cabin door. "He belongs to a friend of mine. She left him here the last time she was aboard."

"She?" The word was out almost before Carrie knew it, and she would have done anything to snatch it back.

Mark's expression didn't give anything away. "My niece. She's five years old."

"Oh, I see." If they gave prizes for feeling like a fool, Carrie was aware that she'd win the contest hands-down. "What's its name?" she asked, trying to fill the awesome silence.

This time his eyebrows did go up. "My niece's?"

"No ... of course not. I wasn't getting personal."

"I think you might be entitled to a few personal questions by now...."

"No, really ..." Her cheeks, already flushed from her long sleep, became scarlet. "I meant the toy."

"The last time I heard, he was called Lyon ... with a 'y.' Her spelling's a little shaky. Why? Does it matter?" Mark tried to keep a straight face but was having a hard time.

"Go ahead and laugh," Carrie said wearily. "I couldn't feel more of an idiot than I do already. Do you mind if I clean up?"

"Of course not. There's a clean towel on the rail in there." He jerked his head toward the lavatory.

"I remember seeing it once before. . . ."

"That's right. I needn't have told you." He was watching as she tried to smooth some of the wrinkles from her slacks. "How do you feel?"

"Like Rip Van Winkle—but better, thank you." The last two words were tacked on deliberately. "Would you mind telling me what kind of a pill you gave me? I'd like to keep a supply on hand. For collectors and door-to-door salesmen."

His glance held hers as he considered his reply. For the first time, Carrie thought in some annoyance, he was really looking at her. Obviously he was not enamored with what he saw; as plainly as if he'd spoken, he was gauging the translucent pallor of her complexion, her mussed hair, and the gray smudges under her eyes.

What she didn't know was that Mark was also noting the perfection of those delicate features for the first time. Even the defiant tilt of her chin as she confronted him couldn't hide the tremulous quiver of softly curved lips.

Sudden guilt made his voice brusque. "Go on in and clean up. You'll be on your way home in no time."

But even his terseness couldn't hide his change of manner, and Carrie was quick to spot it. What's more, with feminine disregard for logic, she resented it. His sympathy was more galling just then than anything he'd done before—even that hard kiss when she'd just come aboard.

She shot another quick glance at him from under her lowered lashes. The way he was behaving now, he'd probably help her across the street and suggest a course of vitamins rather than a quiet date where they could have a chance to really talk.

Mark moved closer and snapped his fingers in front of her nose. When she jerked back, he made a satisfied rumble in his throat. "Thank god. I thought you'd gone into a coma standing up. You're sure that you're all right?"

"*Must* you keep harping on it? I'm fine, I tell you." She brushed past him and peered through the galley window. "Why, we're back at the marina again! When did we come across the sound?"

"While you were asleep. There wasn't any point in hanging around over there. Not with Rudy watching everything we did." As she turned to stare at him over her shoulder, he sighed audibly and said, "I suppose I'll have to explain."

"That's the understatement of the year."

"Okay, I'll make a cup of coffee. You could probably use it."

"What about you?"

"I've had so much coffee that I'm up to here with it." He drew a finger across his throat. "You may not know it, but it's been a long day."

"It isn't over yet," she pointed out. "How am I going to get home?"

"I can drive you and arrange to have the garage

pick up your car. Where are you staying on the island?"

"Don't tell me that's still a secret." She nodded toward her wallet, which was in plain sight on the control panel.

"I get the feeling that a cup of coffee isn't going to be enough to change your mind about me," he announced with some irony. "Would you, by any chance, be free for dinner?"

Carrie had seldom been issued a less enthusiastic invitation. For an instant she wanted to retaliate and suggest a snack at local police headquarters so they could tidily accomplish everything at once. The shadow of that thought must have showed in her face, but Mark's voice was just as peremptory as ever when he said, "Well?"

Carrie tried to match his tone. "Food sounds better than coffee. Have we time to go to the inn so I can change?"

He nodded with some reluctance. "If you like. As a matter of fact, I'm staying nearby."

"Then I'll just rinse my face and comb my hair. It'll only take a second."

When she emerged a minute or so later, Mark had folded the blanket he'd draped over her and put away her pillow, restoring the cabin to its immaculate condition. Only the small suede lion staring down at them from his perch on the shelf added a touch of homely warmth.

"Does he stay aboard?" Carrie asked solemnly.

Mark nodded. "Seems to like it. Besides, with

him around, I don't have to arrange for extra security."

"No problems?"

"Not until today," he said just as blandly. "Ready?"

"I think so." She looked around in some perplexity. "I have the feeling I've forgotten something."

His glance raked over her, and then he grinned and reached down by the foot of the bed. "How about some shoes? The neighbors will talk if you go off without them. Sit down on the step."

She shook her head as if to clear it but did as he ordered. "I can put them on, for heaven's sakes. You don't have to bother. . . ."

"I'm building up some gold stars," he said, kneeling in front of her and calmly putting her shoes on without losing a bit of dignity in the process. "Besides, I took them off, so it's the least I can do."

For some reason, his bald statement did nothing for Carrie's peace of mind. As they moved out onto the stern of the cruiser and Mark turned to lock the sliding cabin door, she pointedly made her own way from the deck to the wharf before he could even offer a helping hand.

The marina at South Beach boasted a few more people than earlier in the day. Two teenagers were sharing a bag of potato chips as they sat on the porch rail of the combination grocery and tackle store, but they didn't even pause in their conversation when Carrie and Mark walked by. Nearby, a pool-maintenance man was loading some equipment in the back of his truck and gave them only a casual glance.

Carrie took a minute to stare over her shoulder at the line of moored pleasure boats along the wharf behind them. "Your friend Rudy seems to have disappeared."

"It was about time—he had a full day," Mark contributed grimly. "Is your car around here?"

"No—it's down on the beach turnoff. Why? Did you want to see it?" She pulled up. "I don't think you believe me, even yet."

"Don't be ridiculous! I thought you might want to get something out of it." He took her by the elbow and urged her alongside a late-model station wagon parked at the edge of the lot. "This is mine," he said, reaching in his pocket for his keys and unlocking the door for her.

Carrie felt a little foolish after her outburst and sat stiffly in her corner while he went around and got in on the driver's side. The engine caught on the first try, and her lips tightened. She should have known that he wouldn't have car trouble—nothing so trivial would dare happen. Then the motor died and had to be restarted before they could reverse, and a faint smile went over her face.

Mark glanced across to see the last of it. "The automatic choke's playing up. I keep meaning to have it fixed," he explained.

She snuggled down into the upholstery and felt more comforted. "At least it works. Be thankful!"

He nodded absently as he swung out onto the

main road and started back toward the north end of the island. "Been down here long?"

"Just a few days." Her head turned. "How about you?"

"Not long ... on the island, that is. I work in Savannah."

"Oh? That's a surprise."

He pulled around a truck loaded with gardening tools and accelerated on the straightaway before asking, "Why is that?"

"I thought you made a living poking around in wet suits and abducting strange women."

"Just on odd Tuesdays." He sounded amused. "Besides, you came aboard of your own free will. Don't forget that."

"I haven't forgotten anything. Incidentally, we're not going to have a very pleasant dinner if you take that attitude. And I'm hungry." The last admission came out in a decidedly thoughtful tone. "At least, I think I am."

He gave her an alarmed glance as he let up on the accelerator. "Not carsick, are you? I can pull over ..."

"Certainly not. I've never been carsick in my life." She rubbed her forehead fretfully as the speedometer needle shot up again. "But I'd like to know what was in that pill you gave me. I have the funniest floating feeling. . . ."

"You just need some food. Breakfast was a long time ago."

"It would have been—if I'd had breakfast. I was going to eat after I'd watched the sunrise."

She rested her head against the back of the seat and stared dreamily out through the car window. "The oaks are pretty in the dusk, aren't they? They look almost black against the clouds. This morning it was the same . . . only when the streaks of color were paler. . . ." Her voice trailed off as she decided to think about it, and her lashes came down.

The next thing she felt was Mark's grasp on her shoulders as he shook her gently and said, "Carrie, wake up. Come on—open your eyes. You're home. We're in the parking lot of the inn. You have to get up to your room."

She smiled idiotically and let her head drop back against what she discovered was the comfortable curve of his shoulder. "Don' want to go anyplace. I like it here. S'nice and warm."

"Carrie, *will* you wake up? I can't carry you up to your room. There's a bellhop with his eye on us right now. To say nothing of the doorman. You'll have to get vertical." The last was said with a firm shake, which made her open her eyes in protest. He pressed on, "Look, all you have to do is put your arm around my waist and move your feet. Can you do that? It's not far to the elevator."

"Elevator." She gave it four syllables and brought her chin up. "What's happened to dinner?"

"Oh, no. Not till you can navigate properly. I'll call room service when I get you upstairs."

There was a pause. Then she said, "I'm not sure I like that."

37

"Like what?" He paused in the middle of opening his door.

"Don't need you upstairs," she said, bestowing a glassy stare. "I can manage m'self."

"I wish to god you could," he said wearily, getting out of the car. "The next time I try the good-Samaritan act when anybody's seasick, I'll head for the nearest psychiatrist." He slammed the door and went around to open hers. "As a matter of fact, I may end up there anyhow."

"End up where?"

"At a psychiatrist's."

Her eyebrows drew together in a disapproving line. "You said we were going to my room ... don' want to go anyplace else. Jus' want to sleep."

"Hey—don't lie down on the seat! We're getting out. Upsy-daisy," he said, pulling her alongside him. "That's the girl. Now, stand there and take a deep breath. Inhale ... way in ... now let it out."

Carrie automatically followed his directions and felt the waves of drowsiness recede as nighttime air coursed through her lungs. A minute later she looked around in puzzled fashion. "How did we get here so fast?"

"You missed a few blocks taking your nap." Mark kept an arm around her shoulders as he urged her forward. "It's nice to have you under the flag again. Which way's your room?"

"That elevator over there, I think." She yawned as he steered her past the flowerbeds.

"Take another deep breath," Mark said, keeping

a watchful glance on her. "I don't want you to drop off again. How long has it been since you had a decent night's sleep?"

Carrie wrinkled her brow, trying to think. "Well, I had to pack the night before I left. Then the flight was delayed because of fog in Savannah. Robbie wanted me to stay over at her house there, but I didn't want to just then. . . ."

"Robbie?" Mark kept his arm where it was and punched the button on the elevator for the ocean-front wing with his free hand.

"Roberta Seymour . . . a friend of mine." She felt his fingers tighten on her arm and glanced up at his stern jawline. "Do you know her?"

"We may have met." As the elevator doors opened, he pulled her inside. "Which floor is your room?"

She closed her eyes to think. "Third."

He pushed another button and held out his hand. "Your key?"

She patted her pockets and brought it out triumphantly, only to have him take possession. "Three-two-seven." He was reading the tag as the self-service elevator shuddered to a halt and the doors opened again onto the covered breezeway of the wing. "It must be down here to the left."

"I could have told you that." Carrie's air of hauteur would have been more successful if she hadn't been clinging to Mark's shirt to stay vertical. "I don't think I'll call the police first thing, after all," she muttered as he swept her along the concrete walk.

"Well, that's good to hear. . . ."

"I'll call them after I talk to a lawyer," she went on, ignoring his interruption. "I've decided to sue you for what you've done today."

"All I did was wash your face after—"

"I *know* when you washed my face," she interrupted, mortified. "I'm talking about giving me that pill or whatever it was."

"How was I to know that you hadn't been to bed for a week before that?" he demanded bitterly, pulling up in front of a louvered screen door at the end of the corridor and putting her key in the lock. "It's no wonder you're punch-drunk." He shoved open the door and dragged her across the threshold of a comfortable room with floor-to-ceiling windows at the end and a double bed against one wall. The navigation lights of two ships heading toward southern waters could be seen through the wide windows.

Mark didn't waste any time admiring the restful green-and-blue color scheme or the teak furnishings. He simply dumped Carrie's limp figure into the nearest armchair and went back to close the door.

She tried to summon some dignity. "Thank you for bringing me home." There was a pause while she searched for something scathing to add about his behavior, and decided to argue about it another time. "You can go now."

A wave of red crept up his neck at her offhand remark. "Thanks a lot."

"Just leave the key on the bureau."

Her lashes had started to descend again when Mark opened the bureau drawer and rapped out, "Where are your pajamas? Or is it a nightgown?" He pawed through a froth of pastel lingerie and held up a lacy slip, only to drop it again with a snort.

His action was as effective as the cold air in the parking lot in getting Carrie quickly to her feet. "What do you think you're doing going through my things?"

"Calm down, honey." He opened another drawer even as he spoke. "You can get ready for bed while I call down for something to eat. Ah!" He gave a satisfied exclamation as he found a pair of pale-blue pajamas. "These will do nicely."

"I'm glad you approve."

He ignored her sarcasm, pushing the pajamas into her hands before he marched her toward the bathroom door. "Go on in there and change. I'll call the dining room for some food." As she opened her lips to protest, he said, "Give up, girl."

"And if I don't?"

"Then I'll put you to bed myself. It wouldn't be the first time today."

She drew in her breath sharply.

"If you're not out in five minutes," he added, "I'll presume you've fallen asleep and come in to get you."

She wriggled away from his clasp and said bitterly, "The hell you will," as she closed the door behind her and turned the bolt with a satisfying click.

"You shouldn't have done that." His voice was amused as it came through the door panel. "Now if you fall asleep, I'll have to call for a maintenance man with a screwdriver to get the door off the hinges."

She put her cheek to the panel and said distinctly; "Anybody would be a welcome change. Go away...."

"Not until I see you safely tucked in, damnit. I'm phoning for food now—so get a move on. Otherwise the waiter will wonder what I'm doing here."

"That'll make two of us," she told him with an audible sniff. Unfortunately his retreating footsteps indicated that he hadn't waited around to hear.

A look at her bedraggled figure in the mirror was enough to make her start shedding her wrinkled clothes. Maybe a quick shower would do something to improve matters.

The feel of hot water on her shoulders was refreshing, but it didn't do much to clear her thoughts. A minute later she decided that more desperate measures were needed, and eased the faucet until the lukewarm spray changed to a cold jet that left her gasping. Thirty seconds of that was enough to send her back out onto the bathmat, reaching for a terry bath sheet nearby.

By the time she'd toweled herself dry, she felt almost human again. She combed her hair and decided to let it hang over her shoulders rather than pulling it back. There was a moment of indecision while she stared at her lipstick. She'd look considerably better with it; on the other hand, she'd hate to have Mark Ralston think that she'd done anything to acknowledge his presence.

She compromised by applying the faintest touch of color, and then decided to use some dusting powder on her shiny nose. The result, she noted with some satisfaction, was worth it.

As she stood there, she rubbed her arms absently, and suddenly realized that she couldn't emerge in thin pajamas. Aside from convention, she was cold. She started to unlock the bathroom door to make her wants known, when she heard the hall buzzer and Mark's footsteps as he went to answer it.

There was the sound of another masculine voice and a cart bumping against the wall as it was wheeled in. Carrie kept her ear to the door, trying to translate the murmur of conversation. Then a strange voice said, "Thank you, sir. Just push the cart outside when you're finished. Sleep well." The last was added as the outer door was closed.

An instant later Mark's palm sounded on the door panel just above Carrie's ear, and she jumped like a scalded cat as he boomed, "Coast's clear. You can come out now."

Just as if he were clairvoyant. Carrie grimaced, but she unlocked the door and put her head cautiously around the frame.

Mark, she saw, had calmly gone back to the

table by the window and was arranging the silver-
ware. He looked up finally when she remained on
the threshold. "Now what's the matter?" he asked.
"Have you gone to sleep standing up again? I
thought the shower would help."

She rubbed her arms over the goose bumps on
her skin. "I'd like my robe, please." As he simply
stood there, she snapped, "You'll have to bring it
to me."

His eyebrows climbed. "Have to?"

"These pajamas are too thin ..." She started
again, "You can't expect me to parade around in
front of a complete stranger ..." His frozen expression softened a little, which proved that he was
enjoying her plight. "Would you please get my
robe in the closet? *And* my slippers," she added,
curling her toes on the cold tiled floor.

"Of course." He moved then and disappeared
behind the closet door, to reappear almost immediately with her sheer wool caftan robe over his arm
and a pair of quilted slippers in his hand. "Here
you are." He turned away as soon as he gave them
to her, saying, "Hurry up, will you? The soup's
getting cold."

Carrie didn't waste any more time. Two
minutes later, she was sitting across the damask-
covered table from him attacking a bowl of mine-
strone as if she hadn't eaten for a week.

"I hope you like club sandwiches," Mark said
when it was time for the next course. "I didn't
think to ask before you were under the shower."

She eyed hers happily. "It looks delicious."

"Good. Pass your cup, and I'll pour some coffee. It might help you stay awake long enough to finish your supper," he added as she yawned before taking a bite of her sandwich.

They ate in amicable silence after that until there wasn't anything left except some decorative parsley. Carrie was even surveying that hopefully when Mark discarded his napkin and leaned back in his chair.

"Feeling better?"

She nodded. "Yes, thanks."

"Don't thank me. I had to sign the waiter's slip with your room number." He lifted his coffeecup in mock salute. "Thank *you*."

"You're welcome," she managed finally. "Sure you don't want to charge me for the boat ride as well?"

"Not this time," he observed. "Roberta mentioned that you had a temper."

"Robbie Seymour?" She sounded dazed. "So you *do* know her. Why didn't you say so?"

"There was no hurry." He stretched long legs past the table and took a final swallow of coffee. "I called her when you were taking a shower. I wasn't sure you were in shape to be left alone tonight."

"But she's in Savannah. That's twenty-five miles away."

"If you're unhappy about the long-distance phone charge, I used my credit card," he informed her solemnly.

"Don't be absurd. I just want to know what you told Roberta."

"I left it sort of vague. It seemed simplest to say you were sleeping things off. . . ."

"You didn't!" Her voice went up. "What on earth will she think?"

He seemed genuinely surprised. "I don't know. What *will* she think?"

"Oh . . . men!"

"Well, it sounds like a damned silly thing to worry about—if you want a masculine opinion. Roberta was just concerned that you were under the weather. She told me you'd been working too hard before this trip." He wrinkled his forehead as he tried to remember. "Something about coordinating productions for a civic opera company. Is that what you do?"

"Close enough." She shot him a suspicious glance. "You don't sing, do you?"

"Practically never." He sounded amused. "Does that help?"

"Absolutely." She rested her head against the back of the blue-chintz armchair. "I don't mind feeding you dinner, but if you'd confessed to being a closet tenor, I'd dump you off the balcony."

The corner of his mouth twitched. "That bad, eh?"

She flushed slightly at his undercurrent of amusement. "Not really. Most of the time I love my job. . . ."

"You don't have to explain. I understand perfectly." He leaned forward. "Can you manage on your own tonight? I told Roberta I'd call her back if you needed help."

"I'm perfectly all right." Carrie's declaration was spoiled somewhat by having to swallow a yawn before she could get the words out.

He got to his feet. "Well, don't try any moonlight walks on the beach."

"I'm not a full-fledged moron." She got up and trailed behind him as he made his way to the door after retrieving his jacket from the back of a chair. "I thought you were going to do some explaining."

"Not tonight," he told her calmly, reaching for the doorknob. "It's such a dull story, you'd be asleep before I started. I'll be in touch with you one of these days." He gave her a friendly pat on the shoulder.

Just the way he would pet a cocker spaniel, Carrie thought rebelliously. She moved to put her slipper in the door as he would have closed it behind him. "When?" she asked baldly.

He stopped and frowned over his shoulder. "You shouldn't be standing in the cold air dressed in that outfit."

"I don't plan to spend the night here. I asked 'when.'"

"When what?" He grimaced. "Now you've got me doing it."

"I want to know when I get the explanation. Otherwise . . ."

"If you're planning dire things, I'd suggest that you wait until tomorrow, when you won't yawn in the police sergeant's face." As he saw her lips harden, he relented. "Okay, so we'll talk. In the next day or so, I promise."

Something in the tone of his voice made Carrie realize that she shouldn't argue further. And there was something about the look in his eyes that made her drop her own glance and step back. "All right."

"Now . . . get in that room and go to bed."

She nodded without looking up.

"Good night, Carrie." He traced a line down her cheek with a gentle finger.

"G'night." Carrie could barely get the word out. "And . . . thank you . . . for everything."

He nodded and was gone, striding down the concrete breezeway without looking back.

As Carrie climbed into bed a few minutes later, she realized that it was probably the first time in history a kidnap victim had politely thanked her abductor for his actions and bought his dinner in the bargain.

Chapter Three

When Carrie opened her eyes the next morning, there was a bright golden sheath of sunshine across the end of her bed, and she glanced toward the window to see a blue sky that looked more like May than December.

Palm trees and sunshine, she thought happily, just like the travel folders. Then the telephone on the bed table rang stridently, and she recalled that it wasn't the first time. Perhaps Mark Ralston had developed a conscience overnight and was calling to tell her about it.

"Hello," she murmured breathlessly, almost dropping the receiver as she tried to sit up.

"Carrie, is that you?" The voice at the other end of the wire was unmistakably feminine.

Carrie's heartbeat thudded back to its normal cadence. "Of course it's me, Robbie," she said. "That's a silly thing to ask."

Roberta Seymour exhibited the patience that accounted for her wide circle of friends. "Not so silly, sweetie. After I talked to Mark last night, I wasn't sure I'd find you still at the inn. Besides,

I've called twice before this morning and couldn't get a response. What's going on?"

Carrie pushed a pillow behind her back. "Nothing. I was sound asleep." She squinted to see the clock on the bureau. "Good heavens! I didn't realize it was so late."

"Now you can see why I was worried. And, of course, I couldn't contact Mark ..." Her voice trailed off.

There was an instant or two of silence before Carrie cut in wryly, "Well, he isn't here—if that's what you want to know."

"Carrie, don't be silly." The other's laugh was infectious. "Discretion is Mark's middle name. If he indulges in any torrid affairs, the women involved aren't talking. Besides, he sounded genuinely concerned about you last night."

"I don't doubt that. ..."

"*What* did you say?"

Carrie recalled that Roberta's blond elegance cloaked an unaffected and fiercely loyal nature. She would undoubtedly find all sorts of plausible explanations for Mark's behavior. "I said," Carrie went on carefully, "that he treated me like a brother."

"It didn't sound like that."

"Well, that's what I meant. I was simply tired out."

"You must have been, if you're still in bed." Clearly Roberta wasn't going to let her off the hook quite so soon.

"I'm getting up right now—so you don't have to worry any longer."

Roberta cut in with the privilege of an old friend. "What do you have planned today?"

Carrie glanced at the face of the clock again and knew in her bones that there was no point in hanging around waiting for a telephone that was not going to ring. Mark Ralston evidently wasn't the least concerned about her threats to go to the police.

"Carrie, have you gone back to sleep again?"

The other shook her head, forgetting that it was a wasted gesture. "Nope, I was thinking. . . ."

"There's no point in spending a day of your vacation doing that," Roberta pointed out with infallible logic. "I'll buy you lunch if you'll come into Savannah. It would be lovely to see you."

Carrie translated that to mean that Robbie wasn't through asking questions. On the other hand, she decided, there were still some things *she* wanted to ask. "All right, I'd love to. But I can't be there until about half-past one. Is that okay?"

"Fine. It might save time if we meet at the Hilton downtown. I'll see you in the lobby at one-thirty."

"See you," Carrie confirmed, and hung up.

It wasn't until a moment later that she suddenly remembered she was without a car. She called Roberta's home number back, but the phone rang unanswered. Evidently Robbie had been calling from somewhere else. "Damn!" Carrie murmured, and sighed before dialing the inn switchboard. "I would like to rent a car," she said when the operator came on. "Do you know who I call?"

"Of course, Miss Shaw. Incidentally, I just took a message about your own car. Shall I read it?"

"Please."

"The garage reports that it should be fixed by late this afternoon, and they'll deliver it here to the inn." The operator went on, "Did you want to rent another car?"

"Actually, I just want to go into Savannah for a few hours," Carrie confessed. "What's the best way?"

"Our regular island bus will be leaving shortly," the woman said helpfully. "Shall I make a reservation for you? They can bring you back here later in the afternoon. Most of our guests use the service."

Carrie glanced at her clock again. "It sounds just right, thanks. I'll be ready."

She emerged from the mini-bus in front of Savannah's famous hotel some time later and surveyed her surroundings with a pleased expression. The old southern city with its gracious squares and high stoop houses had won her affection on the first visit, and it was a continuing love affair. Even now she looked forward to a few more hours in its charming environs.

The tempo on the city street was antebellum, but the modern hotel with its attractive brick entrance was just the opposite. Carrie found Roberta looking into the display window of an art gallery that opened into a corner of the lobby.

She sidled up to her. "How about some northern carpetbags, lady? I can let you have them cheap."

"Carrie!" Robbie spun around and surveyed her affectionately. "You fool! Don't you know we tar and feather people here for talking like that?"

Carrie dropped a light kiss on her cheek. "Sorry. Southern atmosphere brings out the worst in me."

"You can't be feeling very bad if you're acting like this," Roberta said, giving her a top-to-toe look. "I'd say you were back to normal."

"Very much so." Carrie smiled at her with real affection. "It's good to see you, Robbie. You look wonderful!"

Her compliment was absolutely sincere. Roberta Seymour's willowy feminine beauty was enhanced by pale blond hair, skewered, Gibson-girl fashion, atop her head. The old-fashioned style emphasized her lovely profile and a delicate complexion that harked back to an era of hoop skirts and petticoat dresses. Even in her black-velveteen pantsuit, the young Savannah widow fitted into her surroundings as smoothly as the Spanish moss in the live-oak tree gracing the hotel patio. Certainly she didn't look old enough to have two teenage sons at home, Carrie thought. What a pity that Charles Seymour hadn't survived the car accident that had taken him away from his beloved family three years before.

Carrie pinned a bright smile on her face so that

Robbie wouldn't know what she was thinking. "Checking to see what your competition's doing?" she teased, jerking her head toward the art-gallery door.

"How did you know?" Roberta smiled without rancor. "Fortunately there's a good market for historic homes these days, so the Seymour family's still eating."

Carrie knew that the Seymour family would have eaten very well if Roberta hadn't been a talented artist whose watercolors of Savannah scenes had received well-deserved recognition. "I'm glad of that," she said, linking arms with her as they moved out to the street. "You promised me lunch, and frankly, I'm starved. Where are we eating?"

Robbie smiled mysteriously and gestured toward Madison Square. "There's a special place close by you should enjoy. It's only a few blocks, and the walk will be good for us."

The two of them strolled down the shaded sidewalk leading to the historic square named for a president but with the figure of Sergeant William Jasper on the imposing monument. They paused for a moment to read about the hero from the siege of Savannah and then walked on to see the imposing church parish house where General Sherman was quartered during his occupation of Savannah in 1864–1865. As Carrie admired the mansion's ironwork and impressive Gothic carving, Robbie recounted some of the history. "We have to thank Sherman for the survival of our historic homes," she reported dryly. "While Atlanta and most of the other southern cities were burned to the ground, Savannah was saved by the general's intervention. He even wrote to President Lincoln and said in effect, 'Mr. President, I give you Savannah' ... for a Christmas present," Robbie added with a touch of irony. Then her warm nature resurfaced. "But at least the city survived, and we're all grateful for that. It's a terrible thing that I have to tell you about your home state—you should have come back to stay long before this."

Carrie smiled. "I'm not going to stay, even now. This is just a holiday. I wanted time to catch my breath."

"Umm. I'll bet there's more to it than that." But before Carrie could start to protest, Robbie went on hastily, "I want you to see a restoration job on this next block. The windows and doors are in a special color we call 'haunt blue.' It's a pity you can't go in and see the floors ... wonderful old heart of pine that's priceless these days. But at least you can admire the Savannah gray brick they used in the construction."

She swept Carrie along, telling her about the famous bricks that were fired in kilns beside the Savannah River before the industry perished during the Reconstruction period. By the time she finished, they had pulled up in front of one of the city's famed "paired houses," and they were ushered into a crowded eating place on the ground floor.

The room was filled with round tables whose tops were literally jammed with serving dishes.

The tables, in turn, were surrounded by diners busily helping themselves to the succulent array spread out before them.

"This used to be a boardinghouse years ago," Robbie explained. "The cooking became so well-known that the owner opened the place to the public in self-protection. No frills—just marvelous food." She broke off as a smiling young woman beckoned them to two seats that had just been vacated at a nearby table.

"Enjoy your lunch," she said simply, and left them to it.

It would have been hard to do otherwise. Carrie made a dazed count of the dishes available before she picked up her fork. For entrées there were heaping platters of fried chicken or broiled flounder, plus a casserole of macaroni and cheese. Vegetables included green beans, butter beans, yellow squash, and collard greens. In addition, there was a choice of potato salad, cole slaw, or rice and gravy if anyone was still hungry. Pitchers of iced tea were passed around the table at frequent intervals, along with plates of drop biscuits and pots of honey. When dessert brought banana custard pudding or coconut pie, Carrie shook her head feebly.

"How could you do this to me?" she asked Roberta. "I must have eaten four million calories in biscuits alone. You should have warned me."

Roberta merely grinned. "You're not finished yet. Pick up your plate ... we have to take them out to the kitchen. If only I could train my family this way," she added with a sigh.

Once they had deposited their dishes in an immaculate kitchen presided over by a smiling cook, Roberta paid the check and they went outside to pause on the sidewalk.

"I knew you southerners were spoiled," Carrie said, pulling on her blue topcoat and settling a bright silk square at her throat, "but I didn't know how much. Umm . . . that food."

"We just believe in gracious living. When General Oglethorpe arrived here in 1733, his field tent was lined in damask," Robbie said, chuckling, "and we've gone on from there. It's no wonder that you no'therners were determined to hang onto this part of the world."

"I flatly refuse to rehash the battle between the states," Carrie told her. "I'm in such a mellow mood now that you'd win hands down." She looked up the tree-lined street and sighed. "I wish I had time to explore the rest of the neighborhood, but the last Hilton Head bus leaves the airport about an hour from now. By the time I get a cab from the hotel, I'll be cutting it fine."

Roberta consulted her watch and nodded. "I suppose we'd better go right back, then." As they set off down the sidewalk, she said, "You should have told me you were without a car; I could have driven out to the island."

"It wasn't any problem." Carrie pushed the strap of her shoulder bag more firmly on her shoulder. "I had engine trouble yesterday, but the car will be ready tonight."

"Engine trouble?" Roberta gave her a puzzled

look. "How did that happen? Mark didn't say anything about it."

"There was no reason he should. I hadn't met him then. That was how the whole thing started." Before Roberta could frame a query, Carrie plunged on, "How well do you know him, anyhow?"

"Mark?" Roberta smiled slightly as she admitted, "Not as well as I'd like to. And that puts me alongside half the women in Savannah. Mark Ralston started working with the Port Commission here about six months ago. The word got around fast that he was an eligible male ... more than eligible, as you might have gathered," Robbie said in some amusement. "That's why he didn't go unnoticed. Quite a few of the local belles have tried hard, but apparently he wasn't impressed. I understand his sister and her husband have a vacation home on Hilton Head, and he apparently spends his spare time on the island. I think that's where he met Angela."

"Angela?" Carrie's brows drew together as she tried to think where she'd heard the name recently.

"Angela Forza. One of our newer citizens." Robbie's expression didn't give much away, but Carrie knew from her wry tone that she was leaving a great deal unsaid. "Her brother is the main stockholder in a big new firm that opened here last year. They lived in New York before."

The two women stopped at an intersection by the square and waited for a traffic light.

"You were saying ..." Carrie prompted when the light turned green and they started across.

Robbie smiled. "Was I? I thought I'd said it. What else did you want to discover?"

"Where does this ... Angela ... fit in with Mark Ralston?"

"That's what quite a few women would like to know. Angela's appeared on his arm all over town for the last month. She's a gorgeous brunette and doesn't go unnoticed."

"Is he serious about her?"

Roberta started to chuckle. "I haven't the foggiest. Nobody has the nerve to ask. At least he didn't bring her into the conversation last night when he was grilling me about you."

Carrie pulled up in amazement and then started walking slowly again. "Why on earth should he want to know about me?"

"Who can tell? He certainly can't intend to waste his time with a woman who has the most gorgeous figure of anybody I know and a profile that had every man at lunch today sneaking another look."

"They were probably counting the freckles on my nose."

"All five of them?" Robbie nodded thoughtfully. "That could be. And of course, they don't know about that dreadful temper of yours. ..."

Carrie shook her head. "There's nothing like a bosom chum to send a woman's ego plummeting. Seriously, though, what else did Mark ask?"

"Mainly where you came from. How long I'd known you . . . that sort of thing."

Carrie started to laugh. "I hope he wasn't interested in my bank balance?"

"Did he impress you as the kind of man who'd live on his wife's salary?"

"He'd be more apt to throw it in her face before he chained her to the kitchen sink," Carrie admitted.

"The women he's dated around Savannah would prefer it if he chained them in the bedroom."

"Honestly, Roberta . . ." Carrie tried to sound shocked.

"Facts are facts. When you were with Mark yesterday, you must have noticed his attraction. If you didn't . . ."

Carrie surveyed her blandly. "If I didn't . . ."

"Then you really do need a vacation." The older woman turned to look at her. "Frankly, I don't believe you."

"All right . . . so the man was attractive," Carrie admitted. "He was also overbearing, dictatorial, stubborn, and entirely too sure of himself."

Robbie's eyes twinkled. "Surely you can take care of that on your next date. When are you going to see him again?"

"There wasn't anything definite. He owes me dinner, though." Carrie turned her attention to a display of needlepoint cushions in a shop window.

"Then you'll see him." Roberta wasn't misled. "The man's a gentleman, for all his failings."

"I wasn't thinking of those. I'm wondering if

he'll have time to fit me into his social schedule," Carrie said ruefully. "This Angela you were talking about must be taking up most of his time."

"Maybe there was nothing better in view. Mark sounded concerned about you last night. You must have done something right."

Carrie thought back over the time she'd spent being seasick and sleeping in Mark's company. Any spare minutes had been devoted to threatening to haul him off to jail. Hardly the things to put away in a memory book.

Roberta correctly interpreted her woeful expression and patted her arm as they crossed the street toward the hotel. "Never mind. You know what first dates are—sheer horror most of the time." When Carrie didn't answer, she went on, "How did you meet him in the first place?"

Carrie thought rapidly, trying to decide exactly what to mention. When she came right down to it, there wasn't much that could be laundered for repetition. And as charming as Roberta was, she couldn't take a chance on the story being circulated. "Actually, we met on his boat," she began carefully.

"I'd gathered that. Mark told me that you were seasick."

"Oh ... yes ... well ... there isn't much to tell," Carrie finished awkwardly.

Roberta smiled. "I'll accept that for now, but sometime I expect to hear the whole story. It's no wonder you're a rousing success at that job of yours, if you're always this diplomatic."

"I'm not. You should have heard me last week when I found the *Aïda* chorus members playing poker in the freight elevator instead of checking their costumes for dress rehearsal. And the week before, our Wagnerian soprano told me off when her dress got caught on a rock at the back of the stage and she couldn't make her exit with the tenor." Carrie shook her head as she thought about it. "Talk about tempers!"

"It sounds fascinating." Roberta laughed. "I can see why you'd hate to give up a job like that to get married. Is 'Old Faithful' still asking you?"

"That's no way to talk about George. . . . He's a kind, thoughtful person," Carrie said, trying to sound enthusiastic. "I could do a lot worse . . . he's as solid as they come."

"Darling—so's Gibraltar, but it has its limitations. If you'd wanted to marry the man, you'd have done it a year ago."

Carrie kept her glance lowered as they trudged up the steps of the hotel. "Maybe. All I know is that even George's patience has run out. I told him I'd give him a definite answer when I got back. That's one reason I wanted this chance to sort things out."

"And instead of a nice quiet interval, you start tangling with Mark Ralston first thing. Scarcely the patient 'boy-next-door' type."

"That's hardly to his credit," Carrie said tartly. "I think he could learn a few things from George. . . ."

Robbie held the big glass door and motioned her into the lobby. "You don't, you know," she said calmly. "You're just saying that." She looked around idly. "I wonder where the bell captain is...."

A well-dressed man who was just coming from the hotel dining room walked past them with a casual glance and then stopped and turned. "Roberta ... this *is* a surprise," he said enthusiastically as he strode toward them. "I wish I'd known earlier."

Carrie's eyes widened as he smiled across at her even as he caught Roberta's hand and held it. He was of slightly more than average height, with sleek dark hair carefully trimmed. His herringbone-tweed jacket was impeccably tailored, but it was his faintly accented voice which held Carrie's attention. She was sure she'd heard it before. And then, as Roberta said, "Rudy! How nice to see you ..." it all clicked into place. He was the man on the dock that Mark hadn't wanted her to meet.

Roberta put a hand on her arm and pulled her closer. "Carrie ... this is Rudy Forza. And this is Carrie Shaw—one of my dearest friends, who's down here visiting."

"Car—ree." It came out in two long syllables the way he said it, almost reverently.

"How do you do." Carrie wished that she hadn't met quite so many Italian tenors who'd used that intonation with her before. Usually when they were asking permission to upstage a soprano.

"Rudy's practically a neighbor of yours at Hilton Head," Roberta said purposefully. "He and his sister, Angela, have a home down at the south end of the island."

Rudy's expression brightened. "As a matter of fact, I'm on my way there now. Angela and I would be delighted if you'd drop in for a drink soon, Miss Shaw."

"Rudy, dear—you can be a knight-errant before that," Roberta cut in, ignoring the murmured protest at her side. "Carrie's without her car today and could use a lift home."

"I don't want to bother Mr. Forza."

"My dear Carrie, I couldn't be more delighted," Rudy said. "I hate driving by myself. Where are you staying on the island?"

"At the inn. . . ."

"Then I go right by your door." He beamed down on her. "You'd be doing *me* a favor."

There were times to just give up, Carrie decided, and this was one of them. "Then I accept with pleasure."

"Fine." He put a proprietary hand at her elbow. "My car's right out in front. Oh ... Roberta ... can I drop you anywhere?" he added, aware that he'd almost forgotten his manners.

"Thanks, no. I have a phone call to make right now, and after that, my car's parked here in the garage. Enjoy yourselves." She raised a hand. "Carrie, give me a call when you have time."

"I'll do that," the other replied, knowing full well that a complete report would be expected before many hours passed. But she managed a wink as she added, "Thanks for lunch. Next time it's my turn." Then Rudy was urging her forward, and she had to hurry to keep up with his strides.

His car was a green Cadillac with a sleek exterior that matched the manners and behavior pattern of its owner. By the time they'd reached the city limits on the freeway, Rudy had skillfully extracted the salient facts of her background; he'd learned where she'd gone to school, heard about the duties of her job, discussed the size of her apartment, and asked how long she planned to stay on Hilton Head. The only facts he hadn't unearthed were that they'd almost met the day before and that she had a nodding acquaintance with Mark Ralston.

For her part, Carrie didn't do as well. Rudy commented briefly that he and Angela enjoyed life in the south and then extolled the glories of his new cruiser for ten minutes after that. When Carrie managed to turn the conversation back to his work, he was even briefer.

"Small-factory stuff. The dullest sort of thing," he said off-handedly. "It's a family concern ... I just oversee the operation—the sales department is my real responsibility." He slowed to take an exit for the freeway that led to a two-lane road heading east. "I'm not at my best explaining things when I'm driving; I could do it a lot better over a dinner table. Tonight, for example." As Carrie hesitated, obviously wondering what to say, he went on persuasively, "The food at the inn is usually first-rate.

Afterward, if the weather stays good, I could show you my boat. Then I might be able to shanghai you for a day's fishing this weekend."

Carrie couldn't very well tell him that a boat ride was the least appealing invitation she could have received just then. Even a bid to go jogging at dawn in the rain would have been better.

"Of course, if you don't like fishing ... you could just look on. There's nothing like an afternoon in the salt air," Rudy's deep voice urged.

"Well, I could think about it. . . ."

"Over dinner? About seven."

Carrie nodded. "That should be fine." It was as good a way as any to find out what she wanted to learn, she told herself. Besides, she knew very well that it would be pointless to hang around her telephone waiting for Mark to call. A woman could get old before her time, doing things like that.

She shifted into a more comfortable position on the leather seat and let her glance rest on Rudy's profile. His sharp, regular features were straight from an ancient coin, and all he needed was a laurel wreath to complete the resemblance. Unfortunately, he seemed well aware of it. Probably women had been elbowing each other for the last ten years just to get a good look at the line of his jaw.

She continued to stare at him, wondering what made her think he fit the role of a nightclub captain better than a rising industrialist. There was something about his manner ...

"Satisfied?" His glance was still on the road ahead.

"I beg your pardon?"

"I wondered what you'd decided. Did I pass?"

"With flying colors." She made her tone light. "You're sure you don't model for shirts or cigarettes in your spare time?"

He shrugged carelessly. "Maybe I'll have to someday." They were passing some roadside stands that sold bait, pictures painted on velvet, and firecrackers. Rudy jerked a thumb toward them. "Nothing like being versatile."

Carrie laughed. "With a vengeance. I'll have to remember the firecrackers. My boss's son would love a package."

Rudy let up on the accelerator. "We can stop now, if you like."

She shook her head. "Not if I'm going to be ready for dinner on time. I'll be driving in to Savannah again soon, and I can stop then. But thanks all the same."

He nodded agreeably and resumed his speed. The big car ate up the miles effortlessly, and they were soon pulling up in front of the stone-fronted inn.

Carrie glanced at her watch as the doorman approached to open the car door. "Now I haven't an excuse in the world. I'll try not to keep you waiting when you come. Will you call from the lobby?"

"Whatever you'd like."

"That might be easiest," Carrie said with a

smile as she stepped out. "Thank you for the ride."

He nodded briskly and drove off. The big car barely paused before turning onto the highway, and the powerful engine roared as Rudy accelerated down the straightaway.

"Reckon he's in a hurry to get home," the doorman said as he and Carrie moved across the drive to the inn's entrance.

"I guess so." Carrie frowned slightly as she looked over her shoulder, glad that Rudy hadn't driven at that speed when she was in the car.

The young woman at the reception desk handed over an envelope as well as Carrie's key. "From the garage," she said, before Carrie got her hopes up. "The man left your car out in the parking lot."

Which meant that yesterday might never have been, Carrie thought as she trudged up the stairs to her room. Unconsciously, she'd hoped for a message from Mark, and the letdown made her feel depressed and weary.

When she reached her room, she went to the window and stared down at the broad, sandy beach and the Atlantic's gray expanse beyond. To the south, a small Coast Guard helicopter circled lazily around a shrimp boat that was headed for harbor and then moved down the shoreline on its routine patrol. Some wading birds at the ocean's edge rose in flight as the noisy copter passed. They turned inland toward the marshland at the center of the island, their long bodies arching gracefully as they soared away.

Carrie stared at the peaceful scene and then let her forehead rest against the cool glass of the window as she wondered what was wrong with her. She was vacationing in a glorious place with every convenience at her fingertips, and all she wanted to do was weep like a heroine in a soppy modern opera.

By the time Rudy called on the lobby phone, she was feeling considerably better. A lengthy shower and dressing for dinner in her most flattering outfit had done great things for her morale. She took a last look in the mirror at her long sheer wool skirt, rearranged the cowl collar on her blouse, and then caught up a matching shawl as she hurried to the door.

The way Rudy's eyebrows went up when she met him downstairs was a tribute to her appearance. So was his murmured *"Bellissima"* as he took her arm and they moved toward the dining room, whose long windows overlooked the pool and the inner patio.

It all helped, Carrie thought, her cheeks taking on additional color. "I hope I didn't keep you waiting," she said.

"You're precisely on time. Besides, for you"— his grasp tightened—"I would have waited much longer." The last two words were given a special emphasis.

Carrie's expression grew more serene. Whether she approved of Rudy or not, the man was heady stuff. His deep voice with its faint accent could

lend charisma to instructions for filling out an in-
come-tax form.

The dining room of the inn was a pleasing
blend of white-damask tablecloths, the gleam of
silver, and flickering candlelight from sconces on
the papered walls.

A waiter in a starched jacket took their order
for pompano after they'd been seated at a round
table by the window, while another brought two
chilled martinis before Carrie had time to do
more than remove her shawl. She draped the wrap
on the back of her chair and then decided to leave
it on the vacant one next to her. "Seeing we have
this extra room," she said to Rudy with a smile.

For the first time, an uneasy expression passed
over his features. "Actually ... we'll be using
those chairs. I should have told you, but it slipped
my mind earlier. I promised my sister that I'd
join forces with her and her date." A sudden arrival at the far end of the room caught his attention, and he shoved back his chair. "There they
are now." He nodded to a couple following the
maître d' toward the table.

Carrie only had time to notice a curvaceous
brunette in a form-fitting gown of white lace before her attention went on to the young woman's
escort and stayed there.

"You're late," Rudy admonished his sister with
family candor, and then turned back to Carrie.
"My sister, Angela. And this is a fishing pal of
mine that I thought you should get to know. May
I present Mark Ralston."

Chapter Four

Carrie hesitated painfully, unsure of what Mark's reaction would be. Then, as she heard him say "Miss Shaw" in courteous but totally disinterested tones, she knew the die had been cast.

Her voice was just as bland. "How do you do, Mr... Rollings, was it?"

"Ralston." This time his eyes came alive to give warning.

"Yes, of course—Ralston. I'm terrible on names," Carrie replied as the two of them sat down across the table.

"Rudy met Miss Shaw in Savannah this afternoon," Angela told Mark in a high, sharp voice that detracted from her image. "She's just visiting down here."

Her patronizing look made Carrie pause. There were only two reasons for Angela Forza to start putting up "No Trespassing" signs quite so early; either she had the right to stake a possessive claim on her escort, or she wasn't about to let any other contenders try their luck while the contest was in doubt. Carrie dropped her gaze to the stem of the martini glass she held in her fingers. "Quite right. I'm just passing through."

"That's not quite right," Rudy cut in. "Carrie is a friend of Roberta Seymour's." The glance he gave his sister warned her to mind her manners or she'd hear from him later.

Angela reddened and pushed her long black hair back from her cheek with a hasty gesture. "Oh, I'm sorry—I didn't realize. Roberta's charming ... she's been so nice to all of us. Don't you agree, Mark?" Without waiting for an answer, she went on to Carrie, "Mark's a new arrival in Savannah, too."

"Oh?" Carrie turned to survey him solemnly. "Is that where you do your fishing, Mr. Ralston?"

Rudy burst out laughing. "Mark does his fishing on weekends, the way I do. The rest of the time he's busy working at the port offices." He gestured for a waiter. "We've already ordered—you'll have to catch up with us."

Carrie waited until their order had been taken and drinks put in front of them before she said, "Exactly what kind of work do you do at the port, Mr. Ralston?"

Mark turned to frown across the table at her. "We're putting in a new navigational guidance system to handle our river traffic. I doubt if you'd be interested."

Carrie spoke up even as he glanced away. "Oh, but I am," she insisted. "You'll have to tell me why they need such a thing."

Mark's tone was dry. "Mainly because Savannah

is eighteen miles from the mouth of the river, and visiting freighter captains prefer to stay in the middle of the channel. That's why we're putting in the new markers ... Miss Shaw."

"Oh, don't be so formal—please," she said, deciding that one way or another, he was going to pay for overlooking her all day. "After all, we're among friends here."

He kept his polite gaze on her. "Of course, Mary. . . ."

"Carrie," she snapped. She saw laughter gleam in his eyes and found it an effort to say politely, "Maybe you'd do better with 'Catherine.'"

Angela put a possessive hand on his sleeve. "Darling, you'll have to pay more attention."

Even Rudy was regarding him thoughtfully. "You're not usually so absentminded, Mark."

"Sorry, I do better concentrating on speckled trout than women at this time of year." Mark glanced casually across the table. "I apologize, Miss Shaw."

"Think nothing of it. It wasn't important." She directed her attention to the seafood cocktail that had just been placed in front of her. Something told her that she wouldn't win in attempting a confrontation with Mark, and any more attempts on her part would set Rudy to wondering about their relationship.

After that, dinner went smoothly. Angela gradually shed her attempts at sophistication and exhibited a warmth and enthusiasm more in keeping with her Italian heritage. Mark treated her with a flattering deference that made the young woman's dark eyes sparkle. Clearly he had made a conquest there.

Carrie kept a tight rein on her feelings and tried to appear equally enthusiastic when she responded to Rudy's sallies throughout the long meal. After dinner was finished, he insisted on their having a nightcap in the lounge overlooking the ocean. It was a dimly lit room with four musicians blasting away loudly enough to be heard in Florida even without their amplifiers. The only advantage of that, Carrie found, was that she didn't have to attempt any conversation. It was enough to sit with an idiotic grin on her face and try to ignore the headache that was beginning to make itself felt.

Angela succeeded in pulling Mark onto the tiny dance floor a few minutes later. Rudy raised his eyebrows but obviously felt that he couldn't do less with Carrie. She was disconcerted to discover that he hummed in her ear as they shuffled around. She should have been flattered, she reminded herself as she smiled up at him. He was certainly the most attractive man in the room, but regrettably, no one had told him that he was tone-deaf.

They encountered Angela and Mark at the edge of the floor just as the combo edged smoothly, if noisily, into a recognizable fox trot. Clearly the only polite thing was to exchange partners.

Mark's reluctance was only too obvious. So much so that when Carrie was fitted into his grasp and they moved away, even Angela looked pityingly after her.

"You didn't have to force yourself," Carrie told him bitterly.

"I beg your pardon." He bent down so that she could get closer to his ear.

"I said that you didn't have to be so damned enthusiastic."

He straightened and scowled. "What do you expect? It was a fool thing for you to do ... letting Rudy see us together. After all the trouble I went to ..."

"Trouble *you* went to." Anger made her voice almost as high as Angela's. "That's a laugh!"

"Pipe down, for god's sake. And stop looking daggers at me. We're supposed to be casual acquaintances."

"Believe me, that's *all* we are. A friend would have exhibited some interest in my well-being. Roberta was on the phone the first thing this morning."

"I was trying to keep you out of things. ..."

"That's more than evident," she snapped back at him. "Now, why don't you tell me it's for my own good? That's the only cliché you've missed."

"I should have made you see sense yesterday when I had the chance," he began.

At that moment the music rose to a crescendo and then stopped, leaving them stranded in the middle of the floor. They applauded in desultory fashion with the other dancers before going back to the table.

"Just stay out of things," Mark added in an undertone meant for her ears alone. "Otherwise you might find your head unexpectedly parting company with your neck." Her eyes widened, but before she could reply, he'd gone on to Angela at the edge of the dance floor and said, "It's getting late—are you ready to leave?"

She pouted but got to her feet and picked up her bag from the tabletop. "It's not that late. You're spending the night on the island, aren't you?"

"Depends." He was putting a white-mink cape over her shoulders.

Her lips tightened with displeasure. "Honestly, Mark, nobody could pin you down, even on a weather report."

"It serves you right," Rudy informed her. "Maybe Mark has plans that don't include you." The glance he directed toward Carrie was thoughtful.

"Just now, my plans include a full night's sleep . . ." Mark began.

"You make it sound like that's something new and different," Angela said with suspicion.

Mark grinned and put an arm around her shoulders as he directed her toward the door. "I'll tell you all about it on the way home." He paused, and his next words were obviously an afterthought. "It was nice to meet you, Miss Shaw. Perhaps I'll see you again. And, Rudy . . . if the cold weather holds, we might organize a fishing party over the weekend. I hear the trout were going for plugs on the waterway earlier today."

"It would be nice if you showed as much enthusiasm toward me as a weekend fishing trip. . . ." Angela's voice floated back as they disappeared through the glass door.

Rudy shook his head. "She'll never learn. A smart woman would be carrying Mark's bait box. Don't you agree?"

Carrie reached for her shawl and let him put it around her shoulders. "Depends on what she's casting for. . . ."

Rudy threw a bill down on the top of the table and nodded his thanks at the waiter hovering nearby. "You sound almost as cryptic as Mark." He held the door for her as they went into the night air. "You're not an angler?"

She smiled over her shoulder. "Fishing's not my sport. . . ."

"How about boating?"

She was proud of her quick reply. "Not my thing, either. I prefer solid ground."

"That still leaves quite a bit of choice," Rudy said easily as they walked toward the elevator. "If the weather stays clear, there's golf or tennis. . . ."

She smiled. "You're determined to make an athlete of me. I'm on vacation, don't forget. Climbing on the plane to Savannah was about as strenuous as I planned to get."

"There's always a slow nature walk through the center of the island."

The elevator door slid open, and when she

would have turned to thank him, he stepped inside without hesitation and said, "Third floor, isn't it?"

Carrie nodded and followed, letting the door thud closed behind them. As the elevator moved slowly upward, she commented, "You've been doing your homework."

"Not at all. Just keeping my ears open when I called your room." As the elevator ground to a stop, he held the door open for her to precede him down the breezeway. "Now, about that nature walk...."

"Give me a day or so." She kept her voice casual as they pulled up in front of her room and she started hunting for her key. "Actually, I've been a little under the weather since I arrived, so I haven't ventured far afield until today."

"I'm sorry to hear that." He unlocked her door and calmly handed the key back to her. "I thought I'd seen you around the island when I got to thinking about it."

Carrie let her gaze meet his as she opened the door. "I did have a hamburger down at the shopping center the day I arrived."

It clearly wasn't the answer Rudy was expecting. His thick dark eyebrows started to draw together, and then he regained his aplomb. "Maybe that was it. I hope you didn't mind joining forces with Angela and Mark tonight—my sister can be a problem, even if you're in the best of spirits."

"I thought she was charming ... and perfectly stunning."

Rudy ignored that to go on probing delicately, "And Mark?"

"Mr. Ralston?" Carrie's eyes grew wide. "He isn't very sociable, is he?"

Rudy appeared to think that over. "I don't know. I thought you two found quite a lot to talk about when you were dancing. Angela thought so, too."

Carrie started to reply and thought better of it. Just then a gust of wind swept along the concrete breezeway. She shivered and pulled her woolen stole around her shoulders. Fortunately the action gave her the out she was looking for. "Could we discuss it another time?" she asked plaintively. "I'm half-frozen ..."

"Sweet Carrie—forgive me." He pressed a lingering kiss to her wrist, letting her feel the tip of his tongue against her skin for the barest instant. Then, as he saw her confusion at the sensual gesture, he released her hand and stepped back. "Next time, *cara mia*, I'll find a better place for us to say good night. Until then ..." He nodded and strode back toward the elevator. Carrie saw him go and went into her room, carefully bolting the door behind her.

The evening had been so full of surprises that she expected to have trouble sleeping when she got into bed a little later. Therefore, it came as a considerable surprise when she finally opened her eyes to discover pale morning light edging the drapes in her room. A moment later she heard the sound of masculine voices beneath her balcony.

She rubbed her eyes and walked over to peer through the curtains. Below her window, two pool-maintenance men were laughing together as they assembled their equipment for the big Olympic-sized pool. Carrie yawned and checked the time on her travel alarm. Seven o'clock! And she'd thought they were the dawn patrol.

She yawned again and stretched as she padded toward the bathroom to turn on the shower. If she kept on at this rate, she told herself, she'd qualify as a full-fledged descendant of Rip Van Winkle.

When she finished breakfast in the inn's coffee shop, it was just past eight. She walked slowly through the patio toward her room, thinking that the prospect of a day with nothing to do wasn't appealing in the least. Still killing time, she paused to read a bulletin on island activities near the elevator, and smiled as she saw an item at the top. Hotel guests were cordially invited to try their luck in a crabbing tournament that morning at the south-island pier. Equipment, she learned as she read on, would be furnished by the inn's social director.

Her thoughtful gaze ran quickly over the rest of the schedule. A community bicycle ride in the early afternoon left a lot to be desired, as did a nature walk and lecture at sunset. But crabbing! Her lips curved in anticipation. Now, that was the thing! And what a coincidence that Mark's boat was moored at the same pier.

An hour and a half later she was locking the door of her car in the south-island lot and noting that a familiar-looking station wagon was parked nearby.

She zipped her navy-blue down jacket and tied a scarf under her chin as a concession to the season. Her pale-blue denim pants, which completed her outfit, weren't very warm, but they were the only things in her wardrobe suitable for kneeling on a concrete pier while waiting for a crab to come calling.

Picking up a brown-paper bag that the inn's social director had given her, and whistling softly, she put the car key in her pocket and headed toward the dock.

The marina grocery store showed lights in the interior and smoke coming from a chimney, but no customers were in evidence on the broad front porch. Carrie decided December must be a slack time for the yachting crowd, as she made her way down to the edge of the pier and stared at the rows of pleasure boats in their moorings. She let her gaze run swiftly over Mark's cruiser, and her lips tightened with disappointment at its deserted appearance.

She looked around her carefully, ostensibly choosing a place for her crabbing but wondering if there were any onlookers to her actions. The breeze rattled a halyard on the flagpole near the marina steps, but that was the only disturbance.

"Damn!" Carrie said softly to herself. She hadn't planned on getting away from it all with such a vengeance. Heaving an unhappy sigh, she sat down on the cold concrete and reached in her paper bag. She brought out a raw chicken neck that had already been knotted onto a length of stout twine. "Let it down in the water slowly until it just touches bottom," the social director had told her. "With any luck, a crab will catch hold of the piece of chicken. . . ."

"What do I do if that happens?" Carrie had asked, never really considering the possibility of success until then.

"Bring up the bait *very* slowly. Otherwise the crab will get alarmed and drop off en route. You have to be patient." She had looked at Carrie with some amusement. "It's pretty late in the season for this. There may not be any crabs still around. I honestly didn't think we'd have any people, either. You're the only volunteer we've attracted all week."

Carrie thought of the cold December day outside and said, "I'm beginning to think the crabs are the only ones with any sense. But since I've gone this far . . ."

"Well, I'm delighted you're taking part," the social director told her frankly. "How about joining our community bicycle ride later?"

"I'll let you know," Carrie stalled.

"I understand. You want to see how many crabs you catch first."

"Umm. Something like that." Carrie couldn't very well admit that the bait in the brown bag was intended for a far bigger catch, that it gave her a reasonable excuse for being on the south-island pier and the chance to see exactly what Mark Ralston was up to.

"Good luck," the social director had said as she waved her on her way. "I hope you come back with a big one."

Carrie smiled back at her. "Exactly what I had in mind."

In its formulative stages, her plan had seemed foolproof. Now that she was crouched on the hard concrete pier overlooking a deserted row of boats, the obvious disadvantages became apparent.

First off, it was colder than the fringes of the South Pole. She discovered that as she let down her bait into the gray murky water and tried to find a comfortable position that didn't involve instant frostbite for her fingers and derriere. After three minutes' waiting, she raised the chicken neck slowly back up to the surface and surveyed it. Greasy, dripping, and icy to the touch, it left a lot to be desired. Evidently the crabs felt the same way. Grimly she lowered it again and tried sitting tailor fashion until her thighs ached. She shifted onto her knees and risked another quick look down at Mark's cruiser. Still no evidence that there was anyone aboard.

She blew on her frozen knuckles and clutched the wet string. All it took, she told herself sternly, was a little determination.

Twenty minutes later, she had gone through an entire course of isometric exercises and used a bushel of positive thought, but it was no use. By then she was a solid icicle from her waist to her knees, and her toes were beyond caring. She hadn't received a solitary nibble from the crab population, which, considering the weather, wasn't surprising. Any crab with brains was probably sojourning in Palm Beach for the season.

Carrie straightened her clenched fingers and watched the twine slither below the surface without regret. The brown bag was delivered with equal economy into a nearby litter can as soon as Carrie was able to stand upright and hobble over to it.

Then she stood hesitating on the edge of the dock and stared down the line of cruisers. The sensible thing would be to acknowledge her defeat and simply head back to the inn. If she went down to Mark's cruiser and found him aboard—perhaps with Angela or another "friend"—it would be embarrassing and sound the death knell to their acquaintance. Not that their acquaintance was in a healthy state as it was; Mark hadn't been subtle in his remarks the night before.

She hesitated a moment longer and then walked down the pier, as she had known that she would from the beginning. If Mark was aboard and alone, she could mention that she'd been crabbing nearby and thought she'd drop in. It was a thin excuse, but it was the truth, and she had no intention of letting all her suffering go for naught.

A few moments later she drew up alongside the big cruiser and surveyed it carefully. The stern deck looked familiar except for some greasy marks on the white rubberized matting that she hadn't remembered. Mark must not have had time to clean them off, she decided. She glanced over her shoulder, and finding the pier behind her still completely deserted, she stepped onto the afterdeck. Slowly she moved up to the glass cabin door for another glimpse of the interior.

At first the cabin appeared to be in its usual immaculate shape; the upholstered settee was devoid of clutter, the teak bar top was gleaming with polish. Even the carpet . . . Her glance went down to the deep-piled rug and then stopped abruptly. The same type of greasy marks she'd seen on the afterdeck were visible near the galley steps. As her gaze shifted, she saw a small, battered suede toy lying by the baseboard heater.

It was her sleeping partner from the forward cabin. What had Mark called it? Lyon? That was it! And it belonged to his niece.

Then why was it discarded on the rug with one of its suede sides ripped open so that the stuffing trailed out?

Carrie's hand went to the glass door and pushed it aside, allowing her to step cautiously into the cabin. She moved over to the pathetic stuffed figure and picked it up, annoyed that anyone had treated it so badly.

She looked around and swallowed as a sudden thought occured to her. "Mark?" she said quietly. And then more loudly, "Mark . . . are you here?"

A thud suddenly jarred the closed bathroom door—such a violent one that Carrie gasped and jumped a good three inches. When another muffled thumping followed, Carrie paused with her hand on the glass door, temporarily conquering her instinct to set a new sprint record.

Then her common sense triumphed over fear, as she reasoned that any captive locked in the bathroom probably needed help more than she did. The least she could do was unlock the door and find out.

She made sure, however, that the glass door at the stern was pushed ajar so that she could manage a hasty exit if needed. Then she hurried back to the locked bathroom door, where the thudding was still going on with desperate regularity.

As soon as she turned the key and pulled the door ajar, she saw a familiar figure hunched facedown on the floor with his arms and feet bound and a layer of adhesive tape across his mouth.

"Mark! Oh, god! I didn't know ... I didn't dream it was you!" Then, as he drew his knees up for another automatic assault on the door, she leaned down and struggled to turn him over, saying urgently, "Stop kicking, will you! It's me! And I'm on your side, you darned fool. That's what I've been trying to tell you all along."

Chapter Five

It was difficult to see him properly through the tears that were streaming down her cheeks. She scrubbed them away with icy, trembling fingers that smelled of chicken fat and saltwater. Then she was down beside him again, fumbling with the nylon cord on his ankles and murmuring foolish questions like "Are you all right?", "How long have you been like this?", and finally, "Damn, I can't budge this knot!" Even as she saw his eyebrows come together at the last remark, she added hastily, "Just a minute ... I'll get a knife out of the kitchen drawer. Be right back. ..."

She found a paring knife without trouble but discovered that her fingers were trembling so much that she had trouble holding onto it. Taking a deep breath, she steadied herself against the kitchen counter and then hurried back to the bathroom. "I'll start on your ankles," she informed him breathlessly. "I don't think there are as many arteries and things down there. ..."

There was a strangled sound from Mark's throat, and she hastened to reassure him. "It's just a paring knife, and not very sharp." That remark came as she started sawing at the tough nylon line. There was another muffled sound from him, more like a groan that time, and Carrie's cheeks got redder as she tried to ignore it and get on with her task.

Fortunately, the rope parted company before very much of Mark's skin did. "There!" Carrie said in a tone of satisfaction. She would have liked to massage his ankles to improve the circulation, but a strange shyness made her hesitate to touch him. "If you could walk out to the cabin, I could do better cutting that rope on your wrists."

Mark was pushing himself erect even as she spoke, but she had to steady him when he took his first step.

"You've been hurt," she said in alarm, catching sight of a swollen lump behind his left ear. "Oh, lord, you probably shouldn't even be walking around."

Mark growled something and started to shake his head as if he were arguing with her, but the sudden motion made him pale and close his eyes in pain.

Since it was obvious that he wasn't paying any attention to her strictures, Carrie decided she'd steer him toward the nearest mattress.

Again Mark proved to have a mind of his own. When she started to turn him toward the forward bunk room, he stumbled stubbornly through the tiny galley and up the steps into the main cabin.

"That's enough." Carrie half-leaned and pushed against him until he sat down unwillingly on the upholstered bench at its side. "You can't go running around the deck with your hands tied behind you and that tape on your face." She paused and added earnestly, "I'd peel that off, except that it will hurt like the dickens. When I get your hands free, you can do it." She stopped as he shook his head again, slowly but even more definitely than before. "You mean you want me to do it now?" she asked.

This time he nodded, his gaze intent.

"Well, if you insist." She put down the paring knife on the bench beside him and examined the strips of tape across his mouth. "Lord, they've trussed you like a mummy." She thought for a second and then patted his arm. "I'll bet there's something in the medicine cabinet with alcohol ... after-shave, maybe?"

She hardly waited for his slight nod before she was hurrying down to the bathroom, and was back in no time with a small glass container and a towel. "This might be messy," she said, arranging the towel under his chin and starting to pour the after-shave over the tape. After she'd moistened it, she put the bottle and the towel on the counter and said, "Okay, I'll start yanking. Make a noise if you want me to stop."

There were eight separate pieces of tape, and Mark didn't make a sound until the last one had been piled on the bench alongside. Then a steady undertone of profanity rolled forth. When he stopped to take a breath, Carrie said almost tearfully, "But you told me to take it off. I'm sorry—I didn't mean to hurt you. . . ."

"Oh, hell! I wasn't talking to you." Mark sounded so weary that Carrie peered at him in alarm.

"I don't think you should be talking at all," she said. "Not until I get you to a doctor. Turn around so I can untie your wrists."

"Use the knife. . . ."

She shook her head as she went to sit on the other side of him. "I can untie this knot," she said, struggling with it. It took a few minutes, and she broke two fingernails in the process, but she finally said triumphantly, "There! I've got it," and slid the cord from his wrists.

Mark winced with pain as he brought his hands around in front of him and started to flex his fingers. "Thank god! I thought I'd never get free. After I finally came to, I tried everything I knew to loosen that knot." He grimaced wearily. "Do you know that they design marine hardware so there's nothing to protrude? There wasn't one damn thing in that bathroom like a hook or a handle that I could use as a lever."

"So you decided to use your feet and break the door down instead." She kept her voice light, "Those hinges will never be the same again."

"I'd have used my head on it if it would have helped. Only, that felt as if it were coming off already." He touched the lump behind his ear with careful fingers.

"I *think* a cold towel would be good for that," Carrie said judiciously. "But I'm not sure. As long as you've come this far, let's have a doctor decide. Can you walk to the parking lot, or shall I bring help here?"

The wary look that she was accustomed to seeing came over his face. "There's no need for that," he began. "And it isn't that I don't appreciate your efforts, but—"

"I hate to interrupt," Carrie said, doing just that, "but I've heard this song before, and frankly, I'm sick of it. If you think I'm going to disappear into the sunset and leave you here, you're out of your tree. And there's no use arguing with me, because I cut my milk teeth in fights with Italian tenors and their wives."

"Did you always win?" There was a suspicion of a smile on his face.

"Not the first season. But after that, I didn't lose very often."

"Then I'll throw in the sponge." He rubbed his face with an effort. "Right now I couldn't get through even one round without a hand on the ropes."

"Exactly why I suggested a doctor."

"Look"—he sounded as if he were making an effort to be patient—"I'm not even against that. But I'll get there on my own. I don't want you connected with me. You've seen what happened"—he jerked a thumb toward the length of rope—"these people play rough."

Carrie looked alarmed, but only for an instant.

Then she said, "I'm not arguing about that. I'm just saying that right now you need some help. You might be able to make it to the end of the dock, but that's about all."

Mark closed his eyes for an instant and let out a sigh. "Okay," he said finally. "So what do you suggest?"

"That I go to the parking lot and wait for you in my car. If there's nobody around, you let me drive you to a doctor."

"I'd rather be carted to a T-bone steak. I think I'm starving to death."

"You must be in better shape than I thought if you can talk about food at a time like this."

"The day I can't," he said grimly, "you can start shopping for a wreath."

"I'll remember." She got to her feet. "I gather that we're not stopping by a police station on the way."

"You're right." His eyes narrowed. "How did you figure that out?"

"I've been soundly educated by the late show on television. Any upstanding citizen would have been screaming for the sheriff ten minutes ago." She walked to the glass panel and glanced out over the stern. "Sometime you must tell me whose side we're on."

Carrie's use of the plural pronoun didn't go unnoticed by Mark. He opened his mouth as if to protest but changed his mind. "You'd better be on your way," was all he said. "Give me five minutes."

"You'll need a coat. It's cold out there."

"I left my jacket on the forward bunk—I suppose it's still there."

"Then I'll get it for you." She moved quickly down past the galley and slid open the folding door.

He heard her quick intake of breath. "What's the matter?"

There was a pause before she answered. "Either you're a terrible housekeeper or you've been ransacked. The jacket's still here, though."

He moved carefully down beside her, keeping a hand on the wall for support. As he looked into the ravaged cabin, his expression hardened.

"Is anything missing?" Carrie asked in a small voice.

He righted the slashed mattress before he replied, "I shouldn't think so. There was nothing of value for them to find."

Carrie thought of the ripped toy left pathetically on the floor and decided to make some running repairs on that before his niece saw it.

Mark misinterpreted her silence. "I'll tell you about it later. After all this, you deserve some explanations."

"My thoughts exactly," she said lightly. "I'll even volunteer for cleanup crew."

Mark shrugged into his jacket. "The hell with cleaning up. There's plenty of time for that. Go on up to your car—I can manage that far without trouble."

"All right . . . but you'll be careful?"

He grinned. "Honey ... I promise to pull over on the straightaway and let the turtles go past. Now, get going, will you?"

She nodded and went back up to the cabin, carefully retrieving the bedraggled Lyon and tucking him under her jacket before she went out onto the teak transom platform. A quick glance around showed that the south-island pier was apparently still deserted. If there were any onlookers, they were keeping carefully out of sight.

Carrie moved over to the side and stepped across to the dock, hurrying back down past the stalls of moored cruisers and sailboats. When she reached the end of the pier, she went out of her way to skirt the front of the marina store. There was the sound of a radio playing somewhere, but the brisk winter wind was doing its part to discourage dockside loiterers.

Carrie smiled with satisfaction as she passed the flagpole and took the concrete walk leading to the parking lot. There were a few more cars in the marked spaces than when she arrived, but their owners were either fishing or tending to business elsewhere. Carrie unlocked her car and slipped behind the wheel. While she was ostensibly checking her makeup in the mirror on her sun visor, she was able to keep a lookout on the path leading to the lot. A few minutes later she saw movement behind the shrubbery, and when Mark's tall figure came slowly into view, she had started the engine and was reversing to pull alongside him.

She leaned across to open the door. "Get in. There's nobody around that I can see."

He nodded and slid in beside her, pulling the door closed behind him. Carrie was accelerating even as he accomplished it.

"Keep that up, and there won't be any tread left on the tires," Mark groused as he settled back in the seat.

"You must be feeling better—that sounds more like the man who kidnapped me in the first place." Her voice showed that she knew better than to take offense at his comment; that during the last half-hour the emphasis in their relationship had shifted from wary hostility to something considerably more comfortable. "Do you have a doctor nearby, or will you settle for the emergency room of the hospital?" she asked.

"The emergency room will do fine." He half-turned to ask, "I don't suppose we could stop for a hamburger on the way?"

"You suppose right. The doctors might decide to file you away horizontally for the weekend with a diet of crusts and gruel. . . ."

"And you wouldn't want to spoil their fun." He settled back against the seat cushion, taking care to avoid the bruised side of his head. "Women are sadistic creatures. I think you're almost enjoying this."

She bestowed a speaking glance from the corner of her eye but kept her voice solemn. "There was provocation. I haven't forgotten how awful it was to hang over the rail that day."

"All I did was hold your head," he commented mildly.

She shuddered. "I should be glad you didn't need to hold a basin, but that was all that could be said for it. It was pretty shattering for my ego."

"Having you find me trussed like a Thanksgiving turkey isn't any better. Especially locked in the bathroom...." His voice dropped when he remembered another body locked in that same bathroom. "Oh, god," he groaned, "did I ever apologize for that?"

"Not really, but I survived." A faint smile touched her lips, "And you've more than made up for it. So now, why don't you sit back and enjoy the headache you've collected instead of trying to make it worse. I'll poke you on the shoulder when we reach the hospital."

When they drew up by the emergency entrance twenty minutes later, she said, "If you can manage all right, I'll wait out here," suspecting that he would prefer privacy to a chaperon.

His relieved expression showed that she'd guessed properly. "Thanks, Carrie. I'll try not to keep you waiting long."

"The only other offer I've had today was for a community bike ride," she told him dryly, "so don't feel guilty. I have all the time in the world."

He came back through the hospital door about an hour later carefully carrying two Styrofoam cups of coffee. Carrie smiled and rolled down her window to take them while Mark went around to get in beside her. "Very accommodating nurses in this place," he said, retrieving his cup. "I hope I put enough sugar in yours."

She pressed her lips together in exasperation. "If you don't tell me this minute what they said in there, you're going to have a lump behind the other ear."

"Okay ... okay." He raised his coffee in mock salute before he took a swallow. "The general medical consensus was that I have a harder head than a brontosaurus. For the next twenty-four hours, moderation is the key word."

"No pills?"

He patted his shirt pocket. "Only if I start seeing spots before my eyes," he said smoothly. "And a spot you're not."

She gave him a skeptical look. "I won't argue. What's next on the schedule?"

He was staring at her with a bemused expression. "You know, you're really remarkable. Most women would have insisted on playing twenty questions long before this."

She leaned forward to turn on the ignition key. "I'm just being cagey and diplomatic." Then, changing the subject: "Surely you're not planning to go back to the boat now?"

He shook his head carefully. "I'm not that ambitious yet. First off, I'd like a shower and a chance to shave. You can drive me to my sister's vacation place here on the island. She and her family live in Virginia this part of the year." He glanced at his watch. "It shouldn't take me long to clean up—then how about a late lunch date?"

Carrie braced her coffee mug against the steering wheel as she put the car in gear and they moved slowly down the drive. "You don't have to be beholden to me. Probably you should be in bed after all that's happened. I'll take a rain check on the lunch."

"The hell you will. My sister's house is in Harbour Town, if you don't mind detouring by there to drop me off. I'll pick up my car later and then collect you."

Carrie smiled slightly at his reluctance to be driven. It would take more than a women's-liberation movement to quell that ingrained masculine idea. "If you feel up to it."

"I do." Mark drained his coffee and put the empty container on the seat between them. "I must have interrupted a search party when I went aboard this morning. Whoever it was hit me just hard enough to put me out for a while."

Privately Carrie thought that the way he'd been bound and gagged showed more animosity than that. She was wondering why he was keeping it so low-key as she turned onto the main highway from the mainland and accelerated.

Her silence must have given him an indication of her thoughts. "There are easier ways to get rid of bodies on a boat," he went on. "Especially at that time in the morning."

She shuddered and let her emotions override her resolves. "But you just sit there and talk about it!

You don't even intend to report it to the police, do you?"

"No, not now." He paused and then said, "It'll take a while to explain. . . ."

"And I've forgotten all about being diplomatic," she commented ruefully. "All right, it's a struggle, but I'll behave. Maybe we can talk over lunch?"

He solemnly held up his hand. "Scout's honor."

After that their conversation was carefully relegated to safe topics like the weather and how the island population had grown in recent years, until she dropped him off at a sunny villa that fronted on the harbor. When she pulled to a stop in front of the stucco-surfaced home with attractive square bay windows and a crow's-nest addition to the roof, Mark didn't make any attempt to detain her. "I'll call you from here when I leave . . . in a couple of hours or so. Incidentally, I'd rather not hang around waiting for you in the inn lobby."

"Are you sure you even want to be seen in public with me over lunch?"

He took her sarcasm seriously. "There shouldn't be many people around where we're going. Not at that hour. If Rudy hears about it, he'll think I'm just trying to beat his time after meeting you last night."

She wanted to ask how their lunch date would affect his friendship with Angela, but she could see that he wasn't disposed to linger. "All right, then—I'll wait for your call."

After he'd closed the car door, she drove off

without yielding to the temptation to look back. When she reached the main intersection, she turned toward the nearest shopping center rather than heading directly back to the inn. Mark wasn't the only one with secrets; there were some things she wanted to take care of before she saw him again.

One of them was satisfactorily accomplished when she met him at the inn three hours later. She slid in the front seat of his car and waited until he was behind the wheel before she put a tissue-wrapped package on the seat between them. "A get-well present for your niece," she told him as he stared at her, puzzled. "I hope you recover as rapidly."

"Now you've got me curious," he said, reaching down to peel off the wrapping.

While he was doing it, she was able to see that he looked very much better. The shave and shower had worked wonders, and he'd changed into well-tailored gray-flannel slacks and a navy-blue blazer. A close inspection showed that there were still lines of fatigue around his eyes and that his skin was paler than usual, but Carrie could tell that his state of health wouldn't be discussed.

"I'll be damned." He held up the stuffed figure of Lyon and gave her a quizzical glance.

"Your early-morning visitors played rough," she explained as she took the stuffed toy and put it carefully on her knee. "He'd suffered ... abdominal troubles ... when I discovered him. Fortunately there was an understanding seamstress in the leathercraft store at the shopping center."

Mark's reaction was hard to fathom. His glance held hers for a moment, and then he said quickly, "Thanks, Carrie. It was kind of you ... and that's putting it mildly. Now, what about lunch?" He put the car in gear as he spoke.

"I thought you'd never ask." She smiled at him. "Knowing you has been great for my waistline, but I've had a terrible time not gnawing on the furniture for the last hour."

He grinned and turned onto the arterial in front of the inn, heading toward Sea Pines Plantation. "I'm sorry you had to wait—you've been remarkably patient." He edged out into the fast lane of the highway to pass a yellow school bus. "I had to make a phone call before I could do any explaining."

"And they gave you the go-ahead?" As he nodded, she narrowed her eyes thoughtfully. "What did Alice say in Wonderland ... 'it gets curiouser and curiouser'?"

"Sometimes this whole project seems as cockeyed as a trip through the looking-glass. I thought we'd struck out completely until that attack at the boat this morning."

"You mean you were encouraged by it? That doesn't make sense," she reproved. "Maybe they hit you harder than I thought."

"I think I'm still functioning. The reason I couldn't say anything before was that I had to check with the customs people. They're the ones

who got me involved down here in the first place."
As she looked bewildered, he went on. "I told
them that Mrs. Seymour had known you for years,
and after they checked with the authorities in
your home town, you were given a clean bill of
health."

"Well, I'm glad." There was a touch of annoyance in Carrie's tone. "Are you sure all this was
necessary?"

"Unfortunately, yes." His voice lost all traces of
levity. "Despite my best intentions to include you
out ... this morning put you right back in the
thick of things."

"That's a left-handed compliment if I ever
heard one."

"Sorry," he said, although he didn't sound like
it. "For your sake, I'd have been happier if you
hadn't gotten involved, but personally, I was
damned glad to see you this morning."

She smiled slightly. "All right, I'll simmer
down. Tell me more. I take it that you don't
make a life work of installing navigational
guidance markers?"

"Not really—although I could do worse." He
looked more relaxed as he kept the car at the speed
limit heading across the island. "I work for an
electronics company in Pennsylvania. They've
given me time off for this project."

"You mean there's some hanky-panky going on
around here?"

"That's one way of putting it." He kept his
glance on the highway. "It's a known fact that

some of our more sophisticated electronics parts are being smuggled out to Cuba. This alarmed a lot of people in the Defense Department, and they put the heat on our customs men to find the pipeline. In the meantime, experts have been checking the electronics firms in this part of the country for material and supply purchases that don't tally out with final sales figures. That way they can determine if some products are being siphoned off rather than being sold through legitimate channels. The Defense people aren't the only ones concerned," he said with a slight smile. "The Internal Revenue Service is right behind them."

"What does that have to do with the attack on you?"

"Evidently I haven't been careful enough in my nosing around. I've had good chances to check on the waterfront for any unusual cargo operations since I work for the port authorities. Recently we had a tip-off that Hilton Head was being used for the first link of the shipment, with a final transfer out in international waters off the coast."

"That first morning ... you'd just shed your wet suit," she said, remembering. "Were you checking boats at the marina?"

He nodded. "That's what I had on the schedule this morning. Only, when I got aboard mine, I found that somebody had beaten me to it. They apparently objected to my interrupting." His jaw was tight as he continued. "So they took care of me and went on with their business."

"You didn't see who hit you?"

Mark shook his head. "Not really. I remember some kind of movement at the bow, but when I turned around—whammo! After I came to, I'd been stored where you found me."

Her smile emerged. "I can testify that the view isn't great."

"That's an understatement! I kicked on the door for what seemed like a lifetime and couldn't raise a soul. When I finally heard your voice, I couldn't believe it, but I wasn't taking any chances." He gave her a sideways glance. "What were you doing down there?"

Carrie crossed her fingers under a pleat of the rust-and-black-plaid skirt she was wearing with a rust-colored loden coat. "Crabbing," she told him airily. "I heard from people at the inn that it was great."

"This time of year?" He sounded skeptical. "I may not be a native, but even I know better than that."

"Then you should complain to the social director at the inn. She's the one who furnished the chicken neck."

"Complain ... hell! I'm more for sending her a bouquet of roses. I was getting damned tired of that bathroom floor when you came along." He slowed to turn off the highway onto a winding road. "The restaurant is down here a few miles—close to the ruins of old Fort Walker. How's your Civil War history?"

"Not great, but I'm interested in learning," she

admitted. "My folks told me a little about Hilton Head's part in it when I was growing up."

Mark nodded and pointed to another road leading off to the right. "There's a bird refuge through there. It's worth visiting if you're on the island long enough."

He wasn't offering to go with her, Carrie noticed. Nor was he encouraging her to lengthen her stay. Her lips tightened for an instant. "Let's get back to the matter at hand. You mentioned the background for the trouble, but you didn't say what's going to happen next."

There was a pause. Then his eyes raked her sardonically. "That's right. Two reasons. One, I don't know. Second, it's none of your ... affair." The last word was deliberately tacked on.

"Well, *you* got me into it in the first place," she countered. "What was the idea of taking me for that miserable boat ride?"

"Because I didn't want Rudy to see who you were. If you'll remember, our circumstances left a lot to be desired. I *think* we put the dodge over. Did he say anything to you?"

"About knowing you?" She shook her head. "Not in so many words. He said he thought he'd seen me around somewhere, but I'm sure that he hadn't put it all together. He *did* wonder what we'd found to talk about on the dance floor."

"That sounds more like sour grapes than suspicion."

"Could be." She kept her voice casual. "Apparently Angela brought the subject to his attention."

"Angela has an active imagination." Mark kept his eyes straight ahead.

"She's lovely, though, isn't she?" Carrie hated herself for asking a question with such an obvious answer, and then sat there hoping he'd claim not to care for slinky brunettes.

Such hopes were short-lived. "Strictly centerfold," Mark said complacently. "Not much between her ears but a man can't have everything." He ignored the silence that followed and turned left at a fork in the road. "Almost there," he went on a few minutes later. "You can see the widow's walk on the roof from here."

Carrie stared at a white frame building perched on a sloping bank that led down to the gray-green expanse of water beyond. The widow's walk he had mentioned was silhouetted against the sky, looking just like its counterparts on the clapboard houses at Cape Cod. When Mark parked on the gravel drive behind the two-story structure, she could see that someone had hung out a small sign advertising that meals were served, but otherwise made few changes in the old home.

They were ushered through a door which creaked on ancient hinges and led out through the living room onto a porch that ran along the front of the house facing the water. The original screens had been replaced by glass panels, but that was the only obvious change toward modernization. Otherwise worn rag rugs still covered the peg-wood

Of All Brands Sold: Lowest tar: 2 mg. "tar," 0.2 mg. nicotine
av. per cigarette, FTC Report Apr. 1976. **Kent Golden Lights Menthol:**
8 mg. "tar," 0.7 mg. nicotine av. per cigarette by FTC Method.

KENT GOLDEN LIGHTS MENTHOL.
LOWER IN TAR THAN ALL THESE MENTHOL BRANDS.

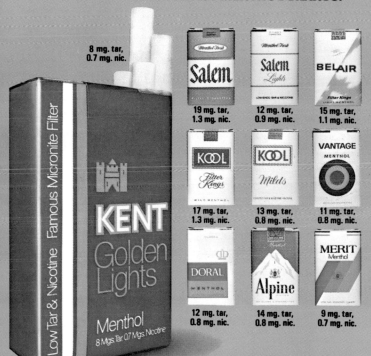

8 mg. tar,
0.7 mg. nic.

Salem
19 mg. tar,
1.3 mg. nic.

Salem Lights
12 mg. tar,
0.9 mg. nic.

BELAIR
15 mg. tar,
1.1 mg. nic.

KOOL Filter Kings
17 mg. tar,
1.3 mg. nic.

KOOL Milds
13 mg. tar,
0.8 mg. nic.

VANTAGE MENTHOL
11 mg. tar,
0.8 mg. nic.

DORAL MENTHOL
12 mg. tar,
0.8 mg. nic.

Alpine
14 mg. tar,
0.8 mg. nic.

MERIT Menthol
9 mg. tar,
0.7 mg. nic.

REAL MENTHOL REFRESHMENT
AT ONLY 8 MG TAR.

© Lorillard, U.S.A. 1976

Parliament	DORAL	Marlboro LIGHTS	Winston Lights	VANTAGE	MERIT Filter
16 MG TAR 0.9 mg. nic.	**13** MG TAR 0.9 mg. nic.	**13** MG TAR 0.8 mg. nic.	**13** MG TAR 0.9 mg. nic.	**11** MG TAR 0.7 mg. nic.	**9** MG TAR 0.7 mg. nic.

STILL SMOKING MORE TAR THAN YOU HAVE TO TO GET GOOD TASTE?

ONLY 8 mg tar

TASTE KENT GOLDEN LIGHTS.

Of All Brands Sold: Lowest tar: 2 mg. "tar," 0.2 mg. nicotine av. per cigarette, FTC Report Apr. 1976. **Kent Golden Lights:** 8 mg. "tar," 0.7 mg. nicotine av. per cigarette by FTC Method.

Warning: The Surgeon General Has Determined That Cigarette Smoking Is Dangerous to Your Health.

floors, and scrubbed wooden tables flanked by bentwood chairs were the reflection of earlier days.

"I took a chance and ordered sea bass when I called for a reservation," Mark said. "Is that all right with you?"

"I think so," she said, slightly confused. "I've never had sea bass."

"You'll like it," their waiter promised. He was a young man in jeans and a white shirt with an immaculate white apron cinched around his middle. "It's right off the boat this morning."

"Then I can't go wrong," Carrie said, returning his smile. "Sea bass it is." When he'd nodded briskly and headed back for the kitchen, she stowed her purse on the chair beside her and glanced across at Mark. "You were right about there not being many people here."

"It's too late in the day—except for the ones propping up the bar," he agreed, indicating a room behind them.

"I'm surprised that you'd risk being seen with me at all," Carrie commented, still smarting from his remark about Angela.

"You have things wrong. It's not *my* neck I'm worried about; yours is the one I had in mind. Now that you know the background, you can give me a wide berth and enjoy the rest of your vacation." He pushed the cracker tray toward her as the waiter deposited steaming bowls of okra soup in front of them.

When the young man left, Carrie said tartly, "What if Rudy puts two and two together?"

"He has better things to do. At any rate your reputation's still unsullied," Mark said, swallowing some soup. "This tastes good."

Carrie possessed a natural feminine reluctance to be shoved aside in favor of cooked okra. "From the way he said good night, I think he has ideas of his own on that score." She had the satisfaction of seeing Mark stiffen at that, and took a swallow of her own soup. "This *is* good, isn't it?"

"Rudy may be great to look at," Mark snapped, going back to the heart of the matter, "but you'd better take it easy. His reputation with the local talent is as long as my arm. Roberta will tell you that, too."

"It's strange she didn't mention it yesterday when she introduced me to him."

"Maybe she had other things on her mind. I'm telling you that the guy thinks he's Tarzan and that every woman he meets is dying to share his vine. You'd better watch your step."

"It's kind of you to warn me," Carrie told him sweetly. "Do you have to worry about Angela, too?"

Mark took a deep breath and pushed his soup bowl away. "I think I can cope."

"I'm sure you can." Carrie was looking up to smile at their waiter as he approached with their loaded plates. "This morning was just an exception."

"Okay, I get the picture." Mark broke off until the waiter had finished his task and left, carrying their soup bowls with him. "I still think I should have dropped you overboard the other day when I had the chance. If I had any sense, I'd be warning Rudy about what *he's* getting into."

"I knew we'd see things the same way . . . eventually." She stared guardedly across the table at him, her thick lashes hiding her triumph. "You're looking sort of gray—I hope some food helps you."

"So do I. I'm surprised I haven't developed a twitch." He picked up his fork and gave her a baleful glance. "I think I just figured out why."

After that, Carrie was content to let the conversation seek a more neutral level as they ate the delicately grilled sea bass accompanied by a serving of southern red rice and a wedge of cornbread. When the dessert course came around, they both succumbed to key lime pie, which was worth a trip to the low country in itself.

"After that, I think a small walk's in order," Mark said when he'd paid the bill and waved Carrie to a side door. "How would you like to see the ruins of the old fort? The Civil War should be safe to discuss . . . if we stick to historical fact."

Carrie adjusted the strap of her shoulder bag and smiled back at him, delighted that he was willing to prolong their time together. From his earlier comments, she was afraid that he would deposit her on the inn doorstep at the first chance. "Some exercise sounds wonderful," she said, strolling beside him on the rustic boardwalk just above the edge of the water. "I've been meaning to visit this site. I can vaguely remember hearing about Fort

Walker from my father when I was a child." She paused to let Mark push aside a tendril of Spanish moss that was hanging over the pathway.

"The only earthworks that are left here now mark the gun emplacements of Fort Mitchel—which was built by the northern forces after the island was captured in 1861." Mark's steps slowed and he gestured toward two big dirt mounds ahead of them. "Their cannons were trained over Skull Creek, but the Confederates never returned. Yellow fever was the worst enemy the Union forces met; the general himself died of it. It's small wonder"—Mark stopped and leaned against the walkway railing—"the northerners constructed a moat around their defenses, and the mosquitoes made the most of it." He looked down into Carrie's rapt face. "Do you know, they even kept alligators in that moat?"

"A live version of the sharpened pikes they used in medieval times." She shook her head wonderingly. "Was the battle for the island a bad one?"

"Bad enough." He stared again toward the water. "The odds weren't good for the Confederacy. There were twelve thousand northern invasion forces massed on a big fleet. The southerners had five hundred men to defend the island, a river steamer, and three tugs."

"I wonder what they thought about when they stared across this water."

"Probably just about what the men on those Union ships were thinking. Or the twelve-year-old 'powder monkeys' in their crews who walked around on the sanded decks." Mark reached for her hand as they started walking again toward the old gun emplacements. "Fortunately most of the southerners had retreated up Skull Creek when the invasion forces finally landed, and the story goes that the Union forces found easy duty here after that. They simply gathered oysters and lived off the land."

"I should think so." Carrie had stopped to read a historical placard by the walkway. "This says drunkenness became such a problem that in 1863 alcohol was restricted to officers only." She started to laugh. "And they were held to one gallon a month."

Mark grinned down at her. "And so ends our history lesson."

Carrie was still chuckling. "We're in no position to criticize. If the sea bass was as good then as it is now, living off the land must have been an unexpected bonanza."

"At least it was a change from 'cracker dowdy.' "

She looked puzzled. "I've never heard of that."

"The colonial soldiers were well acquainted with it. You took crumbs of hardtack, mixed it with water, and baked it. Afterward you fried it in pork fat."

Carrie shuddered. "The sea bass sounds better, thanks."

"I'll make a note of it." He glanced at his watch. "I suppose we should be getting back to the car."

"I hate to leave." She glanced around at the grove of oaks and slash pine with the fringe of palmettos at the quiet water's edge. "This is so peaceful ... like an echo from other times. Even before the days of Fort Walker and Fort Mitchel."

He nodded. "When boatloads of picnickers came down the river from Savannah on a sleepy summer afternoon."

"That must have been fun," Carrie said wistfully as she stared across the quiet water and thought of the picture they would have made. There was nothing to distract her from her daydream; the wind had died except for a tiny breeze, which simply fingered the leaves of the trees and then moved on. The pale winter sun dappled the ground with golden bits and rimmed a blue jay as he flashed into the branches overhead. The surface of the water was without a riffle, and it wasn't hard to envision a river boat full of laughing people with women dressed in crinoline and carrying parasols to guard their complexions from the sun. Beside them, their escorts must have discussed the latest prices for their naval stores and the future of cotton in overseas trade.

Hilton Head had seen it all, Carrie thought. Before the Confederacy, the island had watched English, Spanish, French, and Scots explorers invade its shores, but the lush natural beauty had remained superbly unchanged. As it continued to resist civilized forays even to the present day.

She took a deep breath of the clean salt air and turned to look up at Mark. "Thank you for bringing me here," she told him quietly. "I've enjoyed every minute. I don't think I'll ever forget it."

Mark didn't say anything. Instead he simply took her chin between his fingers, and bending down, laid his lips against hers. The movement was so warm and gentle, so devoid of passion, that Carrie's body instinctively relaxed against his tall form as she kissed him back.

For a moment she thought his mouth started to harden against hers, but he checked himself and pulled away. Only the fact that he was breathing faster than usual gave any key to his inner feelings.

When he did nothing to break the starched silence between them, Carrie managed to say lightly, "I think there's still some kind of a spell on this ground. And now there's an audience besides." She pointed toward two sandpipers on the shore under the walkway.

"Definitely time to leave." Mark maintained a casual touch on her elbow, but he wasn't meeting her glance. "Either that or they'll be complaining about the floor show."

"Then they'd have a nerve. . . ."

He grinned and let his glance linger in a way that brought a flush to her cheeks. "Exactly what I was thinking."

Carrie managed to walk back to the car without giving any more of her feelings away, but she didn't dare look at Mark to see if he was having the same trouble.

They drove back to the inn in silence.

"Will you come up?" Carrie asked when he stopped in the parking lot alongside the ocean-front wing.

"No, thanks." He sounded brusque as he reached across to help her when she fumbled with the door handle. "I may have a lump on the head, but I still have some wits about me. And when I let things get out of hand on a public boardwalk, then I damned well know better than to see you to your bedroom."

He waited for her to scramble out on the sidewalk and turn to face him. She swallowed but couldn't think of a thing in reply.

Mark simply nodded as if he understood all too well. "There's something I'd better tell you," he went on.

Carrie's heartbeat speeded up unaccountably as she drew in her breath with anticipation. "What is it, Mark?" she asked.

"Just that this is as far as we go."

"I . . . I don't understand. . . ."

Her halting words made him frown and say even more roughly, "Look—don't make me spell it out. What happened this afternoon just shows that it'll be better for both of us if we call it quits now. There's no point in dragging out an impossible situation. Have your holiday, Carrie—and then go back home where you belong. Forget about all this. Believe me, that's what I'm going to do."

As she still made no response, he cleared his throat and went on in that level, deep voice, "I'm honestly sorry that things got out of control this way. I should have known better." For an instant he looked as if he'd like to say more. Then his jaw hardened. "But that's the way it is—the way it's got to be. And don't get any bright ideas about changing my mind, because you won't get one damned bit of help from me."

With that, he nodded and drove rapidly out of the parking lot.

Carrie stood where he'd left her and watched with stricken eyes until he disappeared from sight.

Chapter Six

It was provident that the phone was ringing when Carrie unlocked the door of her room, because otherwise she would have yielded to her desire to sink on the bed and give way to the tears flooding her eyes. It wasn't often a man told a woman to get lost or go fly a kite—not when he'd just kissed her in a way that said something else entirely. Unfortunately Carrie had learned enough about that particular man to realize that he meant exactly what he said. If her phone did ring from now on, he wouldn't be on the other end of the wire.

So it was with considerable reluctance that she went to pick up the receiver; her other acquaintances in South Carolina were distinctly limited, and just then she had no desire to talk to any of them.

"Hello," she muttered, trying to blot away the tears with the back of her hand.

"Carrie?" Roberta Seymour asked doubtfully. "Is that you?"

"Oh, Robbie." Carrie's tone warmed appreciably, thinking how nice it was to hear a familiar and trustworthy voice. "I didn't know it was you."

"I'm glad. For a minute I felt as welcome as an overdue notice from the gas company. What's the matter . . . did I waken you?"

"No, of course not. I just came in from lunch." Carrie managed to reach a handkerchief and dabbed at her nose to keep from sniffing.

"Lunch? At this time of day? Don't you feel well?" Robbie pursued the subject with the freedom of an old acquaintance. "You don't sound as if you felt well."

Carrie didn't know whether to laugh or keep on crying at that. She finally chose the former. "Look . . . it's me you're talking to. Not Jeff and Mickey," she said, naming Robbie's two sons. "And if you go after them this way, they're going to ask to be put out for adoption any day now."

Roberta's soft chuckle came over the wire. "Sorry, love. I guess I did forget for a minute. Is it anyone I know?"

"Who?"

"The man who took you to lunch, naturally."

"How do you know it was a man?"

"You wouldn't have just been coming in this late if it had been another woman."

"That's the most ridiculous piece of reasoning I've ever heard," Carrie sputtered.

"Uh-huh." The other woman merely sounded amused. "Who was it? Mark or Rudy?"

"Well, Mark . . ." Carrie admitted reluctantly.

"But I met a good-looking man at the car-rental office down the block the other day, so you'd better add him to the list."

"There's no need to get upset," Roberta said. "You can tell me all about it if you drive in for lunch tomorrow. There's a new place down on River Street that's supposed to be good. You could see the restorations they're making in the port area, and we could browse through the shops down there."

Roberta's magic words "restorations in the port area" made Carrie stop and think. If Mark was employed by the City Port Authority, his office was probably close by River Street. And while she'd been given her marching orders to avoid him on Hilton Head, he couldn't legitimately object to her presence in Savannah. Her eyes narrowed as she thought of the possibilities.

"If it takes you this long to make up your mind," Roberta told her, "then I'm beginning to understand why you have such late lunches."

"Sorry—I was just thinking. I'd love to come."

"Good! I'm almost sure I can make it," Roberta added, "but there's an outside chance a New York gallery owner might come to town. He wasn't able to fix a firm date. . . ."

"Well, don't worry about it. We can always take a rain check on the lunch in that case."

"All right. Let's fix a definite time tomorrow."

"I'll call you," Carrie confirmed. "It's my turn."

"Fair enough. We'll talk then."

Carrie put down the receiver and wandered over to the window. The brief conversation had raised her morale, but it was hard to keep it from sagging again. The trouble was that she had too much time to think. At home, her job was demanding, and any emotional flings she'd encountered had been short-lived through necessity. None of those experiences, however, had involved a man like Mark whose impact on women should be measured on the Richter scale along with disasters of epic proportions.

She stared bleakly out onto the broad beach in front of her and then reached up to rub her forehead. This wouldn't do, she decided abruptly. She turned away from the window and crossed to her closet to get a jacket. A walk on the beach would be good for her disposition. After that, she'd look for an entertaining novel at the inn gift shop.

Her change to jeans and a windbreaker took very little time, and she was soon hurrying down the outside stairs adjusting a scarf over her hair. By the time she passed the edge of the inn property and crossed through the ribbon of salt grasses in the dry sand, she knew she'd made the right decision. The broad beach stretched invitingly on either side, deserted except for a boy and his dog far down to the south. The late-afternoon sun had disappeared behind a few thin clouds, but some warmth still lingered in the air.

Carrie moved through the dry sand carefully, trying to keep it out of her canvas shoes, and then lengthened her stride as she reached the packed damp sand farther down. The tide was starting to turn, but she soon discovered a wide lane of shells still free from the oncoming waves.

Her steps slowed as she surveyed the fascinating shapes and sizes of the shells spread out before her. All thoughts of a brisk walk vanished as she bent over and started searching for colorful finds.

It wasn't long until both of her jacket pockets were bulging, and she was wishing that she'd brought a bag or something more satisfactory for storing her treasures. She was in the process of pulling off her head scarf for a depository when she heard a male voice hailing her. Glancing up, she saw Rudy striding toward her, looking overdressed on the beach in wool slacks and sports jacket.

"I *thought* I recognized you," he said in some annoyance as he finally reached her. "You're hard to find."

"I didn't know I was lost," she replied mildly. His unexpected appearance should have been flattering, but her initial reaction was one of disappointment; the shell hunting had been such fun that she didn't welcome an interruption.

"Well, when I didn't have any success phoning your room, I finally got the desk clerk to admit that she hadn't seen you drive off." He grinned triumphantly. "That didn't leave many alternatives, so I decided to try my luck on the beach."

Carrie stared back the way he'd come, surprised that she'd wandered so far from the inn boundaries. "I'm sorry that you had to go to so much trouble. I started out for a walk and then discovered all these marvelous shells." She reached in her pocket and brought some samples out on a sandy palm. "Do you know anything about them?"

"Not much." He moved closer, but she noticed that he didn't touch any of them. "Just looks like the usual stuff to me."

"At home, the only way we can collect shells is to order steamed clams at a seafood restaurant. This is a great improvement," she told him tartly.

"Hardly in the same league," he admitted, sounding more human. He surveyed her collection again and singled out a smooth gray shell about an inch long. "That's an olive . . . the pointed one next to it is an auger . . . those fat beige ones are called oyster drills, and that white one is a friend of yours from the midwest—common garden-variety clam."

His thinly veiled amusement made Carrie wish that she hadn't mentioned the subject in the first place. Her cheeks took on added color as she stowed her new collection carefully back in her pocket. "You sound like quite an expert."

Rudy either missed her withdrawal or chose to ignore it. "Not really. If you live on the island, shell collecting is a favorite topic of conversation. Even if you're not particularly interested. Angela's always bringing home a pocketful . . ." His mouth settled in an annoyed line. "The trouble is, she doesn't take them out of her pockets, and they don't do a damned thing for washing-machine motors."

Carrie's lips quivered. "I'll remember that."

This time he didn't miss her faint sarcasm. It seemed to irritate him. "I don't know how we got stuck on this topic," he said, dusting his fingers carefully before shoving them in his pockets. "If you want an expert on shells, there's some sort of a naturalist who works here on the island—he's always giving lectures to the tourists."

"I'll check at the desk." Carrie turned to retrace her steps along the beach. Rudy strode alongside her.

"I don't have much time," he said, consulting his watch. "Angela's arranged some sort of a neighborhood cocktail get-together, and I promised to put in an appearance."

"Then don't let me keep you. . . ."

He ignored that. "I'd invite you along, except that you wouldn't know anybody. That can be awkward all around."

His casual assumption that she'd drop everything to accompany him made Carrie's temper start to steam. "That's quite all right. I'd made other plans for tonight anyhow." She managed to keep her voice pleasant but emphatic. Not for anything would she have admitted that her schedule consisted of curling up with a good book.

Rudy nodded and went on, overlooking her annoyance. "I came over to see if you'd like to spend tomorrow on my boat. The weather man says there should be some sun, and the two of us could manage alone in decent weather."

"What kind of a boat is it?"

"A thirty-eight-foot Down Easter with a cutter rig," he said casually.

Carrie gave a soundless whistle. "Your manufacturing business must be good."

He shot her an intent look. "What makes you say that?"

"I'm impressed, that's all. My acquaintances generally run to dinghies or rowboats."

"My boat's not much longer than Mark's cruiser."

Carrie wasn't ready to be caught. She widened her eyes. "Does he have one around here, too?"

Rudy put a hand to her elbow as they moved into the deeper dry sand near the inn boundary fence. "Yeah, I thought you knew. Down at the south marina on the pier next to mine. You were there the other day, weren't you?"

Carrie looked up with a blank expression. "Maybe, My island geography's pretty hazy. I'd have to look at a map to be sure."

Clearly her response wasn't what he expected, but he brushed it aside. "It doesn't matter. Tomorrow's what I'm interested in—not past history. Can you make it?"

"I'm sorry"—Carrie tried to sound as if she meant it—"but I made a date with Roberta a little earlier. I'm driving into Savannah to meet her for lunch."

"Can't you get out of it?" His voice was impatient.

"Not if I want her to speak to me again."

"If I'd known you were so hard to pin down,

I'd have made other arrangements." Rudy's expression showed he wasn't accustomed to being refused. "When will you be free?"

"It's hard to tell," she stalled.

"The day after tomorrow?"

"I think so." Carrie couldn't think of a valid excuse, so she tried to concoct a flimsy one. "I should warn you. I'm not much of a sailor."

"That shouldn't be a problem—we'll find something else to do." There was a satisfied look on his handsome features again. "I don't think you'll have any complaints."

Carrie found herself thinking about Rudy's comment the next day as she drove through the outer reaches of Savannah en route to her lunch date. It was a pity that he was one of those men who didn't improve on continued acquaintance. After being dazzled with his profile at first meeting, Carrie had decided that his personality was all surface gloss with nothing underneath. He pursued unattached women the way Genghis Khan looked for new territory to conquer; it was simply the spirit of the chase that mattered. And Carrie surmised that once Rudy could raise a victory banner over the female in question, he'd be off for more exciting fields.

Not like Mark Ralston, she told herself. Now there was a man who didn't even bother to enter the competition. In fact, he seemed to actively fend off female aspirants—like the Black Knight of King Arthur's time who unseated his challengers on the first joust and then rode off, hiding a yawn behind a mailed fist.

At least Rudy was more flattering to a woman's morale, Carrie decided as she turned toward the river and searched for a parking space. While there would be nothing noteworthy to remember after a date with him, by the same token, there would be nothing painful to forget. An intelligent woman would simply enjoy his profile and close her eyes to his imperfections.

Roberta agreed with her when Carrie broached the idea over lunch. They were seated in a replica of an early colonial tavern, which was somewhat overdecorated, but the food was good and the coffee even better. The older woman took a sip of it before she said, "Frankly, I think you're being a little hard on Rudy. It seems to me he's showing darned good judgment when he asks you out." She let her glance wander over Carrie's turquoise dress worn with a perky silk scarf of blue and green at the stand-up collar. "If you wore that dress the last time he saw you, I'm not surprised he wants another date."

Carrie smiled but commented dryly, "Two dollars will get you five that you've named the only reason. He likes life-sized Barbie dolls."

Roberta's blond eyebrows climbed. "What's so different about that? Most men do."

"At least they hide it better."

"Meaning Mark, I suppose?"

Carrie pushed back her plate with an impatient gesture. "Hardly. He doesn't even bother to be civil." Her glance fell to the tabletop as she went on thoughtfully, "Or maybe he just prefers brunettes."

"A la Angela Forza." Roberta nodded. "That's a strange and wonderful relationship—as they say in the greeting cards. I wouldn't think she was Mark's type."

Carrie's response was prompt and hardly ladylike.

"I mean it," Roberta reproved her. "Mark's not the kind to be taken in by a set of measurements. After about ten minutes of listening to her conversation, I think he'd be long gone."

"Don't underestimate those measurements." Carrie was morose. "And when Angela remembers to be quiet, she hangs on his arm and stares at him like he's a newly certified miracle. It's absolutely disgusting." A small "meowr" floated across the table at that, and she nodded reluctantly. "You're absolutely right—I'd like to scratch her eyes out."

"Good! I like an honest answer." Roberta's attention suddenly focused on the window next to their table, which overlooked River Street. "Talk about coincidence—there's Angela now. She has a man with her, too."

"I'm not surprised." Carrie didn't bother to look, but her voice was dull. "Is it Mark?"

"Nuh-uh. Someone older . . . heavier set." Robbie screwed up her forehead. "I wish I could place him."

Carrie found suddenly that she was curious after all and leaned forward to peer through the window. "He must be a good twenty-five years older than she is," she said, surveying the stocky, well-dressed man who was leaning down to talk with Angela as they moved through the crowds on the popular Savannah street.

Roberta shook her head. "That isn't gray hair—he's just very blond. I recognize him now. It's Jason Wright. His picture was in the papers a few weeks ago. He's a high-priced lawyer from New York who was called in to defend some case. . . ." She rubbed the side of her nose as she tried to think. Then her face cleared. "I know. It was Rudy's company or some competitor of his in electronics."

Carrie watched the two go out of sight before she turned back to Roberta. "What kind of a case?" she asked idly.

"Zoning, I think. Or was it pollution?" Roberta shrugged. "I honestly don't remember. My mind's like a sieve on those things. Why? Is it important?"

"Not really," Carrie bunched her napkin and put it on the table. "Angela must have impressed Mr. Wright enough on his first visit that he came back again. Unless he's involved in some other case. . . ."

"Not that I've heard of." Roberta was checking her lipstick in the mirror of her compact. "Frankly, I would think Angela could do better. That one has a face like the commandant of a Prussian guard. You know the kind—with a dueling scar on one cheek."

"How ridiculous! He's probably very nice as well as being brilliant."

"Well, he's certainly found someone decorative in Angela, and nobody's ever accused her of a staggering IQ—so there's no competition." Roberta got up and pushed back the chair.

"On the other hand, she's probably tired of profiles after living with Rudy," Carrie said, picking up the check. "That's why she welcomes a man with an honest double chin."

Roberta started to giggle as they made their way to the door. "All the ingredients for instant romance. If I hear that anything comes of it, I'll let you know." She paused on the threshold of the restaurant to pull on her gloves. "I *wish* I didn't have that darned appointment. You're going to stay and look at the shops, aren't you?"

"For a few minutes." Carrie wished she could ask if Mark's office was nearby, but didn't dare.

If Roberta noticed her preoccupation, she attributed it to other reasons. She smiled sympathetically. "It's hard to go window-shopping and remember your budget at the same time."

"I'll try to be strong."

"Not too strong. It isn't much fun that way. Thanks for lunch."

Carrie watched Roberta's trim figure disappear around the corner of an old stone building before she set out down the row of shops fronting the river. According to Roberta, they had been part of a master restoration plan. City authorities had salvaged the iron-railed balconies and refurbished the old brick buildings to transform the area into a new Savannah visitors' attraction.

Carrie enjoyed the surroundings as she wandered; even the cobblestones under her feet took on added importance when she read that they had been brought as ballast in the early sailing ships and later put to practical use. She turned a corner and looked up to see a connecting bridge which led to upper-level offices of Factors' Row—named after the cotton brokers who molded much of the city's heritage. Then, as her glance came down again, she saw that she had turned into a picturesque but dead-end street with only one craft and gift shop opening onto it. A few steps beyond, a mini-park softened the brick wall that closed off the street ending. Angela and Jason Wright were deep in conversation right next to it. Even as Carrie noticed them, they half-turned to make their way back to River Street.

Without stopping to reason why, Carrie stepped inside the doorway of the tiny craft shop and bent over a display case. But then, as luck would have it, the couple pulled to a standstill opposite the shop doorway and continued their discussion.

"Could I help you?"

While Carrie had been watching the scene outside from the corner of her eye, a maxi-skirted saleswoman had emerged from the back of the shop and was viewing her with interest.

"I'm . . . I'm not quite sure." Obviously Carrie couldn't continue to stand and stare into the shop's one display case much longer without arousing the shop owner's suspicion. On the other hand, if she tried to leave, she would walk right into the couple outside. Another glance showed that they apparently planned to stick around as long as the cobblestones.

"Was there something special you wanted?"

The saleswoman was viewing her with definite hostility now. Carrie decided that any minute she'd probably check the headlines on the morning paper to see if any of the city's mental patients had escaped overnight. The safest thing would be to buy something and drag out the purchase as long as possible.

"Well, actually, this was what caught my eye," she said, pointing to the first thing she saw in the showcase.

The saleswoman beamed. "That's one of our most popular items, and completely handmade here in Savannah. It appeals to children of all ages."

"Oh, really." Carrie blinked and then looked down again to see what they were talking about. She found that she'd chosen a foot-long stuffed hippopotamus covered in red chintz with white daisies and adorned with false eyelashes like a Hollywood starlet. The result was so patently absurd that she started to laugh.

"Shall I wrap it for you?" the woman wanted to know, briskly taking it out of the case.

"If you would, please." Carrie finally caught a glimpse of the price tag dangling from the hippo's ear and swallowed before reaching for her purse.

Indulgences came high when embroidered with daisies and eyelashes. "Would you take a traveler's check?" she asked, keeping her voice low in case it carried outside the door.

The shop owner frowned again, wondering at the hushed tone. Then her forehead cleared as she saw Carrie pull out her traveler's checks. She was clearly willing to put up with personal idiosyncrasies if it moved the merchandise. "Of course, madam. Box or bag?"

"I beg your pardon?"

"Do you want this"—she indicated the hippo—"in a box or bag?"

"Oh." Carrie cast another furtive glance outside the door. Angela and her lawyer friend had completed their discussion, but they still stood unmoving by the doorway. Even as she watched, Angela reached up with one hand to grasp his lapel and look at him soulfully.

"Is there something wrong, madam?"

The saleswoman's rasping question made Carrie jump. "No . . . no, everything's fine," she babbled. "I was just trying to think. If you could put it in a box . . . maybe with a ribbon around it."

"Certainly. There's no charge for ribbon, but if you want special paper . . ."

"No, thanks," Carrie reassured her. "A ribbon will do fine." She added under her breath, "And take a little longer."

"I beg your pardon?"

Carrie started to explain and then changed her

mind. The simplest thing to do was sign the check.

The saleswoman gathered it in as efficiently as the armful of hippo and disappeared past a beaded curtain into the back of the shop.

Presumably in search of a ribbon, Carrie thought, and hoped that it would take a while. She should have specified polka-dot ribbon or something with daisies to match the chintz. Despairingly, she moved over to the side of the doorway and stood in the shadows.

Angela's words came through the quiet air in a breathy rush. "I'm glad we won't have to pretend any longer. You don't know what this last month has been like, Jason."

"Well, it's almost over now, and we owed it to Rudy." The man's voice was a deep bass, an actor's voice. The intonation was mellow, with every syllable distinct, and Carrie didn't wonder any longer at his success in the courtroom. The possessor of a voice like that didn't need a profile. "Two more days," he went on after a pause, "and we can lead our own lives. If Rudy doesn't like it . . ." Carrie looked out in time to see his shoulders shrug under their expensive suiting.

"That's easy for you to say." Angela's tone showed she wasn't completely convinced, although it was clear that she wanted to be. "He doesn't have control of *your* money."

"Don't worry about that. I've *told* you"—the attorney sounded impatient—"just leave the details to me. Leave everything to me."

Angela continued to cling to him. "Darling, you know I want to. For the rest of our lives."

His features softened, but he merely brushed his mouth over her lips before looking at his watch. "We'll have to go."

"I suppose so. You've double-checked everything?"

"I told you I did." To Carrie's infinite relief, the lawyer put his hand under the girl's elbow to urge her on down the alley. "There's no visa needed where we're going. Keep your passport with you, and . . ." His voice faded away as they walked around the corner on River Street, out of sight.

Carrie moved cautiously into the middle of the shop doorway and stood there for a moment, frowning as she stared after them. Then absently she stepped outside, determined to give them plenty of time to disappear into the crowd of shoppers.

"Madam! Your package . . . your change!"

The indignant hail caught her before she'd taken a half-dozen steps, and she turned to find the shop owner standing in the doorway holding an enormous ribbon-wrapped box. The woman raised it as if she were offering a gift to royalty. Carrie had time to notice the box was big enough to contain a live baby hippo instead of its stuffed counterpart before she guiltily retraced her steps. "I'm terribly sorry," she said, accepting a handful of change and trying not to stagger when the box was transferred to her arms. "I don't know what I was thinking of."

"That's all right, madam. I hope you'll come back again." Without waiting to see how the insincere platitude was received, the saleswoman scurried back into her shop and this time locked the door behind her.

Carrie achieved the safety of her car without encountering Angela or her lawyer friend and drove back to the island with the box containing the hippo on the seat beside her.

In her room at the inn she undid the ribbon and removed the lid of the box. She stared in at her plump purchase and shook her head, wondering what had possessed her. Obviously the hippo would have to be disposed of before she caught a plane back home—either that or she'd be forced to leave her clothes behind. She fingered the animal's ridiculous eyelashes and wondered who she could give it to. Roberta's teenage sons would think she'd lost her mind if she appeared with it in Savannah. On the other hand, Mark's young niece might be enchanted to have a flowered hippo on her toy shelf along with a recently restored Lyon.

She frowned thoughtfully. The package would have to be delivered so that Mark wouldn't suspect her motives. Certainly she couldn't tell how she made the purchase in order to avoid confronting his favorite girlfriend while she was saying a fond farewell to what seemed to be *her* favorite boyfriend. It would be nice to know whether

Mark was aware of Angela's extracurricular interests.

Carrie stared in the mirror at her sandy-haired reflection, wishing that she possessed Angela's startling brunette beauty or Roberta's elegant coloring so that Mark would have thought twice before saying good-bye.

"You're an idiot," she told herself after thinking about it a moment and remembering the way Mark had kissed her at the old fort. There hadn't been anything wrong with the magnetism that had flared between them. It had been right and beautiful. Mark had chosen to ignore it *and* her because of some quixotic notion. "Damn!" she said aloud and walked over to put the lid on her hippo. Maybe by tomorrow she'd figure out how to present it to a reluctant uncle.

Unfortunately, the next morning dawned without any inspiration in the interval. Carrie's mind was as empty of ideas as the sky of clouds. She took ten deep breaths on her balcony to nudge her thinking processes, and when that didn't help, sought solace in a waffle and two cups of coffee.

The phone was ringing in her room when she returned, and she hurried to lift the receiver.

"Carrie?" It was Rudy's voice, more brusque and hurried than his usual treacly tones. "It's a good thing I caught you. I'm sorry about our date, but something's come up, and I'm afraid I won't be able to make it."

Even the two cups of coffee hadn't helped

enough. There was a distinct pause while Carrie tried to think of suitable regrets.

Rudy wasn't prepared to wait. "Carrie . . . are you there?"

"Oh, yes . . ."

"Did you hear what I said?"

"Yes, of course."

"Well, why didn't you say something?" He sounded aggrieved. "I couldn't help it. We can get together later on."

"Heavens, don't worry about it. You took me by surprise—I'd just come in the door."

"Oh?" His voice changed to suspicion. "Where've you been?"

"Breakfast." Carrie was beginning to understand Angela's sudden desire to leave home. "Do you approve?"

"You *are* annoyed." There was a tinge of triumph underneath his words. "Don't worry, my sweet. I'll call you as soon as I can."

Carrie had to smile—he had misunderstood completely. "Of course. Call when you have a chance."

She heard the noise of a kiss come through the receiver and wrinkled her nose in distaste before hanging up firmly. When Rudy called again, she'd have an excuse ready. Life was too short to indulge his monumental ego.

After spending the morning on the beach, she came back to the inn and added some new specimens to her shell collection, which was now threatening to overflow one end of her suitcase. The space limitations made her decide to spend the afternoon in another hobby. She read the list of activities posted on a bulletin board when she emerged from lunch and decided bicycling offered the most advantages.

The social director supplied her with a map of bicycle paths and offered elaborate instructions for an easy afternoon's exploring. "If you go down past the academy and around Gator Point, you can detour by our forest preserve. No one should visit Hilton Head without touring around it."

Carrie looked doubtfully at the distance involved. "I'd just planned on riding in the sunshine for a while. It's such a pretty day."

"All the more reason for taking the nature walk in the preserve. You can leave your bicycle at the entrance—no one will bother it."

Carrie bent over the map. "I wasn't worried about that," she said quite truthfully. "How long does this nature walk take?"

"Just as long as you want. There are signs all along the way that are self-explanatory. You won't have a bit of trouble."

She sounded just like Rudy, Carrie thought dismally, wondering how she managed to surround herself with such forceful acquaintances. "Well, if you feel it's too good to miss . . ."

"Oh, I do."

The woman was so positive that Carrie didn't have the nerve to argue, and later was glad she hadn't. It was pleasant to ride on winding paths under sun-dappled trees, past well-manicured golf courses. The warmer temperature made it a lazy afternoon, and most of the people she saw were moving at a pace as relaxed as hers. Around four o'clock she found herself next to a restaurant with a brick-flagged terrace and decided that a cup of coffee would give her a chance to rest while she planned her route back to the inn. She parked her bike in a stand at the side of the building and made her way around to the front. As soon as she went through the gate, she almost stumbled over Angela, who was sitting by herself at a round table.

"Hello," Carrie said in surprise. "I didn't expect to see any familiar faces in this place."

Angela flashed a welcoming smile. "I did. Rudy asked me to see how you were doing. He felt bad about canceling your date."

There was sisterly concern in her tone, and Carrie found herself wondering what prompted it. She hadn't shown any interest the night they'd met, and from what she'd overheard on River Street, the girl couldn't wait to leave Hilton Head. So why was she pretending now?

Angela went on, paying no attention to Carrie's puzzled face. "He thought I might show you over the island. Visitors often miss the best parts."

"Well, thanks," Carrie said, sitting down wearily in a chair across the table from her. "Right now my muscles feel as if I'd explored every last nook and cranny already." She looked up suddenly. "How did you know where to find me?"

Angela smoothed the front of her red-sailcloth jacket. "That wasn't difficult. The social director of the inn told me that you'd probably be around this part of the island. It seemed simplest just to wait here until you showed up."

Carrie started to laugh. "That woman's positively clairvoyant. The only place she's been wrong was on the crab tournament, and they must have moved out in the middle of the night without telling her." Noting Angela's uncomprehending stare, she shook her head. "It's not worth explaining."

"Whatever you say." Angela beckoned a waitress. "Could we have more coffee here, please? Do you want anything with it, Carrie? I can recommend the macaroons."

"That sounds good," Carrie said, weakening. After the waitress had moved off, she confessed, "I was going to be strong and stop eating for a while."

"I can't see why." Angela gave her an appraising glance. "Men like something to hold onto," she said, without bothering to couch it in polite terms. "At least, that's what I've been told." Her satisfied expression made Carrie think that all of Angela's informants had been men. She could only hope that Mark wasn't one of them.

Angela didn't notice anything amiss. "Have you been to the nature trail yet?" she asked, pushing the cream and sugar within reach when the coffee was served.

"Not yet." Carrie tried to keep from sounding guilty. "The woman at the inn told me all about it, though. I must get there sometime soon."

"There's still plenty of time this afternoon." Angela looked at her watch to make sure, and then went on briskly, "It won't get dark for an hour or so yet, and I can take you over there. I'll even go through part of it with you."

"That's kind of you, but I have my bike outside. . . ."

Angela brushed that off. "What difference does that make? I have a station wagon, and we can put it right in the back. Afterward you can ride back to the inn, and I can drive home."

Carrie tried another angle. "There's no need for you to go to all that trouble. I think there's a naturalist who gives a guided tour if a guest requests it."

"You don't want to hear all those statistics—sometimes he goes on for hours." Angela took a final sip of coffee and pushed away her cup. "Finished?"

"I guess so. If I don't leave pretty soon, I'll eat that last macaroon, and I've already had two." Carrie saw Angela extract a pen from her purse and reach over to sign the check.

Before she could protest, the other woman had pushed back her chair and said, "Rudy has an account here," as if that was all the explanation needed.

"Then you'll have to thank him for me," Carrie said, trying not to sound annoyed. She decided there was nothing else she could say, since Angela was already halfway to the gate and clearly expected her to follow.

Angela superintended the stowing of Carrie's bike into the station wagon, and barely waited for her to slide in the front seat before she started the car. "The forest preserve is about two miles down this road," she said a minute later as she swung to the right onto a dirt trail. She was forced to lower her speed or risk tearing the bottom out of her car on the dirt crown between the tire tracks. "They could do some maintenance on this and improve it, but the horsey set objects every time they bring a road grader around."

"I didn't know it was a bridle trail as well." Carrie was hoping that there wasn't any unsuspecting horse and rider beyond the sharp curves that Angela was still taking faster than necessary.

"They don't have much business in the winter, but it's wall-to-wall horses in the spring. I can't stand them myself."

Carrie's lips twitched. To a casual observer, Angela's comments bore a great similarity to Marie Antoinette's. As the car lurched on through the pine and oak trees, she glanced out the window to say, "This seems awfully deserted for being right in the middle of the island. Aren't there any homes around here?"

"Of course not. The developers had to agree to leave the central part of the island in its natural state before the original owners would sell." Angela gestured with one hand. "A little farther along, you'll see the salt marsh. Of course, that's beyond the old rice fields."

"How big *is* this forest preserve?"

"I don't know." The other's tone was careless. "Miles, I suppose."

"Then how do you find your way around?"

"There are signposts." Angela threw her a faint smile. "Not worrying about getting lost, are you?"

"Well, it is sort of late...." Carrie paused as Angela slowed to turn off onto an even fainter track leading through a pasture where the grass was brown and sparse. "Is this the way?"

"Of course." Angela was sounding impatient again. "You don't have neon signs on a forest preserve. There's the first marker over there." She nodded toward a length of sagging board fence just ahead of the car. "If you park your bicycle there, it should be safe enough. There aren't many people around at this time of year," she added as she pulled up alongside and turned off the ignition.

Carrie looked at the faint path that disappeared in the thick shade under a growth of oaks festooned with Spanish moss. The open reaches of the pasture around her seemed suddenly like a wonderful place to stay.

"Aren't you going to unload your bike?" Angela asked pointedly when Carrie made no effort to move. "I'm sorry I can't deliver you back to the inn, but I just haven't time."

"That's all right." Carrie opened the door beside her and swung her legs to the ground. "I'm surprised that you can take this long. Most people planning a trip have to spend the day before packing—I know I do . . ." She broke off, aware of her gaffe, as she caught sight of Angela's face.

"Who told you that I was planning to go away?" The other's words cut ominously through the silence.

Carrie tried to think of a plausible lie and, as usual, failed utterly. "I saw you yesterday in Savannah," she confessed. "I couldn't help over-hearing."

"I'll bet." The other made no pretense of friendliness. "Did you tell anyone?"

"Certainly not." Carrie's chin came up. "It was none of my business. Besides"—her voice did some cutting of its own—"I don't know anybody who'd be interested."

"Rudy, for one. I should think that would be obvious." Angela got out of the car and came over to watch Carrie unload the bicycle. "I'm sorry," she said finally. "I didn't mean to snap your head off. Jason and I . . . he's the man you saw . . . have tried so hard to keep our trip a secret. I don't think I could stand it if anything went wrong now."

"You don't have to worry about me."

"I'm glad of that." Angela apparently had no intention of dwelling on the subject. She went back to the station wagon and carefully locked the doors, saying over her shoulder, "Are you going to be warm enough in that jacket? It's pretty shaded in the thickets."

"I'll be fine." Carrie didn't plan to linger long

enough to get cold. If she had to take a nature walk, it was going to be a brisk one!

"Whatever you say." Angela paused beside the rustic signboard. "This tells about the history of the preserve, but I can give you that as we go along. There's tremendous variety in the vegetation," she went on, waving a hand toward the grove of slash-pine trees ahead of them. "You'll find bayberry bushes growing under these. Later on, there are stands of oak, magnolia, even hollies."

Carrie blinked in amazement. Angela's glib commentary about the natural attractions on the island was at such variance with her lacquered exterior that it was hard to reconcile the two. Like finding a centerfold beauty working as a den mother between appointments.

"Take this Spanish moss," Angela was going on authoritatively, "it provides great nesting material for the birds around here."

"What kind of birds?" Carrie asked, looking up to see, and then lowering her glance as she stumbled over a rut in the path.

Angela didn't miss a stride. "Owls and woodpeckers here. They go after insects that damage the trees. In the swamp and marshy areas, you'll see ospreys, wood ibis, blue herons, and American egrets if you're lucky."

Privately Carrie wondered if she'd manage to cover that much territory in two weeks, let alone one visit. She decided not to mention it, saying instead, "I had no idea you were such an expert on all this. You didn't mention it the other night."

Angela shortened her stride to give her a side-long glance. "Rudy isn't very interested, and I've never asked Mark." Her lips curved. "We always had other things to discuss on our dates."

As calmly as possible Carrie said, "You might have been surprised. Mark looks like a man with a variety of interests."

"Possibly." Angela was clearly skeptical as she pulled up by another sign, where the faint path divided. "This leads down to a cattail marsh, but we can skip it this trip. There are more interesting things ahead."

"Fair enough. Cattails are old hat—even in my part of the country."

"Jason was telling me that most people don't appreciate them. He says that the Indians made flour from the pollen in that sausage-shaped head," Angela expounded, turning onto another path. "The roots were good for stews, and there's some kind of asparaguslike vegetable you can make from the stems."

"Maybe *he* could, but I couldn't. . . ."

Angela ignored that. "Jason also said that even today they can use the stem fiber for rush furniture and the seeds as pillow stuffing."

Carrie suddenly understood the source of Angela's knowledge on the forest preserve. "Jason apparently knows a great deal about all this."

"Oh, he does!" Angela's tone was reverential. "He knows about everything," she continued, turning left at another sign by a group of palmettos.

Carrie tried to read quickly as they went past. Spanish moss was a member of the pineapple family and an air plant, she discovered, not the parasite people imagined. Its rain-soaked weight often caused branches to break. . . .

Her preoccupation brought forth a reprimand from Angela. "We'll have to keep going if we make the circle tour," she said tartly as Carrie caught up with her. "The light's fading fast."

"I wasn't paying attention." Carrie looked around at the thick vegetation edging the path on both sides. "You'd think they'd clear around the trails better. Without the signpost markers, it would be easy to miss the way."

"A natural look is the whole object," Angela parroted. "Jason says that even the boardwalks aren't necessary. If people care about the land, they should be able to risk the discomfort of the low areas. We're heading toward that part now."

Carrie wanted to ask if Jason would offer to re-place the shoes she was going to ruin. Even then her soles were sinking into the soggy ground, and it was only a matter of time until her feet would be in the same fix. Her annoyance made her forget diplomacy, and she said, "If Jason feels so strong-ly about things, he certainly should be able to handle Rudy. Why all the secrecy about your rela-tionship? It isn't as if you were doing something illegal."

Angela stopped abruptly. "Of course not," she flared, "but you don't understand Italian families. Since my father died, Rudy's the man who makes the decisions in ours. It isn't that he doesn't like Jason," she added, walking on. "It's just that he thinks I'm not old enough to be serious about anybody. That's why he approved of Mark. . . ."

"You've lost me there. . . ."

"Mark doesn't want to get serious about any woman at this point. He told Rudy that the first time he ever took me out. In a polite way, of course." Angela's eyes became thoughtful slits. "My brother believed him. . . ."

"But you didn't?" Carrie held her breath waiting for a reply.

"I'm not sure. Mark says all the right things to a woman, but I don't know if he meant any of them." She turned to survey Carrie. "What do you think?"

This time Carrie wasn't about to make a mistake. "I hardly know the man." Then she shrugged. "At any rate, I think your Jason sounds better. There's a lot to be said for dependability, and from the way he looked at you—you don't have to worry about affection." She stopped and reached down to fish a pebble from the side of her shoe. "Could we rest a minute? I've nearly reached my limit, and I know that my shoes have—we must have walked two miles, at least." She held up a soggy foot to illustrate. "Let's turn back."

"Not yet," Angela protested. "You're not five minutes from the prettiest part of the preserve. After you've come this far, it would be a shame to miss it."

"But the light's almost gone. . . ."

"That's the best time. The waterfowl are spectacular. Jason says—"

"I know . . . I know." Carrie laughed and held up a hand. "I'll take your word for it."

"Good. You won't be sorry." Angela checked her watch. "I should be on my way, though. I'm late now for an appointment."

"Of course." Carrie felt a stirring of unease and looked around to check her bearings. "But are you sure I can't miss the path on the way back? I don't want to spend the night here," she said, trying to make light of it.

Angela glanced at her pityingly. "There's no trick to it at all. You saw the sign markers we followed. Just retrace the route, and you'll be back at the entrance in no time. Even if you missed a fork, each trail is laid out on a loop arrangement that takes you there." She smiled and added, "Cub-scout troops come in here all the time."

"I get the message," Carrie said dryly.

"Well, then, I'll go ahead. Rudy will be in touch with you in the next day or so." Angela gave her a casual wave and was soon out of sight.

Carrie stood where she was, staring after her. Then, as the silence settled, she took a deep breath and turned toward Jason's promised land.

At that moment, as she trudged down the squishy path, she would have happily traded Angela's Jason for one knowledgeable cub scout. Then she chided herself for imagining things and tried to appreciate the scenery around her. She spared a moment to lean over and touch a fat lighter stump with its heartwood core. The sign said that colonials had used the wood in making their fires because of the concentration of pitch. That made her more aware than ever that the afternoon shadows were taking on an ominously dark hue. Much later, and she'd find herself wishing that she had a heartwood torch as well. The disquieting thought stayed with her as she moved on past the stump and followed the track a few minutes longer. The sight of another signpost made her lengthen her stride—maybe she was nearing the viewing spot Angela had promised.

The first words of the signpost were enough to send her hopes plummeting. They announced baldly that walking time for the Waterfowl Pond Loop was fifty-two minutes. If that weren't enough, the sign also reported that alligators and occasional snakes were found in the area, so walkers must stay on the trails.

Carrie couldn't have been more horrified if she'd been confronted by a hot lava flow surging down the path. She whirled to survey the underbrush and swallowed mightily when a tiny bird fluttered through a palm frond. Then she started back along the trail at a dog trot.

As she hurried along, her thoughts were keeping pace. Fifty-two minutes indeed! If she'd gone fifteen minutes more, she would have been stranded in the dark on the damned path, and she could have spent the night hoping that the alligators had gone south for the winter along with the crabs.

Angela had either misquoted her mentor or they'd been completely unaware of time. Carrie shook her head angrily and tried to ignore the stitch in her side.

When she came to the first fork in the path, she reached over to shore up the signpost, which looked like a leaning tower of Pisa. Carrie made a mental note to tell the social director at the inn so it could be fixed, and moved along the left-hand path toward the entrance.

It must have been ten minutes later that she saw a signpost rimming the trail ahead of her and gave an inward sigh of relief. For the last hundred feet or so, the path had turned so muddy that she was wondering if she'd missed her way, since the trail and cleared areas around the clumps of palmettos and oaks looked amazingly alike.

She kept her glance on the signpost ahead, hoping it might show a shortcut to the entrance. When she finally drew up in front of the small placard, it took a moment or two for the horrid reality to seep in. Then she read the words again, hoping she might have been imagining things the first time around. Unfortunately, the words "fifty-two minutes for Waterfowl Pond Loop" and "alligators and snakes" remained defiantly positive. So did the familiar "stay-on-the-trail" warning at the end.

Carrie rubbed her face with a trembling hand as she tried to think. Maybe there were two signs like that—maybe this marked an alternate trail that led to the entrance. But even as her hopes rose, her eyes lit on the stump to the left of the path—the fat lighter stump that she'd seen before.

She shook her head despairingly. All she'd done in the last few precious moments of daylight had been to go around in a circle—still as far from the entrance as ever. And unless a downright miracle was in the making, the alligators and snakes who lived in the neighborhood were about to gain an overnight guest.

Chapter Seven

The hours that followed would always stand out in Carrie's memory as the ultimate in discomfort.

As darkness settled like a shroud around her, she reluctantly moved over to sit on the broad, fat lighter stump. She propped her soggy shoes up on the wood beside her and hugged her knees to her chest. Any self-respecting alligator who wasn't hibernating surely wouldn't be fool enough to start climbing stumps in the dark, she told herself. And the snakes . . . There her mind panicked. What in god's name *did* snakes do? In the movies, they clung to vines and waited to throttle unsuspecting victims. Did they also lurk under Spanish moss on a live-oak tree? Carrie drew in her head as she thought about it, hoping to present less of a target.

In that position, it wasn't long until her neck ached, and then her back. She moved her shoulders and sat there hoping the aching muscles would turn numb eventually, like her cold feet. The wind rustled through the trees around her, and the stiff fronds of the palmettos nearby rasped against each other in mild protest. Carrie pulled her collar up over her ears and wondered if anybody in the whole wide world would notice her absence. When she concluded that nobody would, at least until the inn housekeeper reported her unoccupied room the next day, a suspicious moisture formed in her eyes. Then she discovered she wasn't even equipped to cry, because she didn't have a handkerchief and had to use her sleeve as an emergency blotter.

She decided to stand up on the stump and move her arms and legs for exercise, hoping that it would take her mind off things like roast beef and hot coffee and cheeseburgers and chocolate cake with raspberry filling. If a clump of Spanish moss could live on air, she could certainly manage to do the same thing just overnight.

She finished her bout of calisthenics and was trying to rearrange herself on the stump's unyielding contours when a disturbance in the distant brush set her heart pounding. The vision of an alligator suffering from insomnia flashed in her mind, and she stood up quickly on her perch, intent on putting all the space possible between the ground and her wet feet. They were so cold at that moment, it was doubtful that anything would make an impression on them—even an alligator's bicuspids—but there was no use tempting fate. She was dwelling ridiculously on that thought when a call that had nothing reptilian about it came booming through the brush.

"Carrie! Carrie! Can you hear me?"

She stared into the darkness, so startled she was

unable to speak for an instant. Then she yelped, "I'm over here! Don't go away!"

"Who's going away?" came the cross male voice in reply. "Can you see my light? Shout out when you can!"

"I can't see a thing," Carrie agonized. "You must be going the wrong way."

"Then I'll turn around. Just take it easy."

By that time Carrie had recognized the voice, and the sudden acceleration of her heartbeat had nothing to do with her recovery.

"Mark!" she called hopefully, to make sure. "Is that you?"

"That's right." There was no mistaking the irony in his tone, even over the yards. "Can you see my lantern yet?"

"No . . . this miserable underbrush is so thick . . . wait! Hold it there—I can see it now." Her voice rose with excitement. "I'll come to you."

"Stay where you are! You can break your neck thrashing through this stuff. . . ." There was a crack when a tree branch gave way, and the rustle of dried leaves on the ground, and then he was miraculously there beside her.

Carrie hardly gave him time to deposit the lantern on the stump before she had launched herself against his chest and felt his strong arms close around her.

"Hey . . . that's enough," he said a moment later. "There's no point in both of us suffering from the damp." He pulled a handkerchief from his pocket and started to carefully mop her cheeks. "My shirt'll be wet wash if you don't cut that out."

Carrie took the handkerchief from him and blew her nose. "I'm sorry. I don't know what came over me—I didn't cry before. At least, not much," she amended. "I didn't have a handkerchief."

"Well, I'll make you a present of that one if you like. Sort of a security blanket until we get out of here." He kept an arm around her shoulders as he raised the lantern and located the path. "C'mon, let's go. I imagine you've had enough of this place." Then, as an afterthought: "You *can* walk, can't you?"

"Of course. Why shouldn't I be able to?"

Mark urged her forward even as he said, "There had to be some reason for your being in here." When he felt her body stiffen, he went on, "Don't stop to argue now. You'll be lucky if you don't catch a roaring cold from this experience as it is."

"Will you listen! I *did* try to get out. I even skipped the waterfowl pond that Angela recommended because I thought I was running out of time. But somehow I took the wrong fork in the path and circled back. Only by then it was dark...." She felt his quick intake of breath. "What's the matter? What did I say wrong?"

His voice was a deep rumble. "I don't see how you could get lost. The signs in this place practically spell things out. Even visitors who don't speak English go through it all the time. All you have to do is follow the arrows."

If Carrie hadn't been so tired, she would have reached up and hit him. As it was, she said through clenched teeth, "I *know* what the signs said. I read every word and followed their damned arrows. That was part of the trouble. But I don't think they're in such great shape. The one down at this fork needs to be replanted before it topples over in the mud."

Mark brought the lantern up as they passed a shrub overhanging the path, and she could see the frown on his face. "I don't understand it. Usually this place is in great condition. And what did you mean about Angela? What does she have to do with all this?"

"Nothing directly. She left hours ago, before I got lost."

"You mean she was in here with you?"

"Why, yes." Carrie tried to ignore the icy water that cascaded over her shoe as she stepped into a puddle. "Actually, it was her idea—coming here today. I thought she was the one who'd sent you after me."

"No—you can thank Roberta for that. At least, indirectly. When I talked to her a little while ago, she mentioned that she'd tried to phone you but the people at the inn said you'd been gone all afternoon. I checked with the social director there, and she said you'd planned to visit the preserve on your itinerary."

"*She* planned it," Carrie interrupted with some bitterness. "I didn't."

"Be thankful the woman works late and has a

good memory." His steps slowed as the lantern illuminated the fork in the path and the signpost that Carrie had mentioned.

"You see, it *is* tilted," she told him in a tone of triumph. "Not that it matters, but somebody's been careless."

"More than you think." He went over and pulled the wooden post from its soggy footing with an angry motion.

"Mark—you shouldn't! The next people through here will need that...."

"Not if they ever want to find their way back to the entrance." He carried the post a few feet past the fork in the path. "That's where it belongs," he said in a tight voice, showing Carrie a rectangular depression in the soft ground. "But unless you were familiar with this place, you wouldn't know it. I owe you an apology." Mark shoved it back into its accustomed place and returned to her side. "Now I'm wondering how this all happened." He urged her along the path, keeping abreast when the vegetation permitted and going slightly ahead to light the rutted track when it narrowed.

"That makes two of us." As they emerged in a cleared area, Carrie shivered against the wind, which was flattening the grass around them. "I wonder if Angela got home all right."

"There was music in the background when she called me a little while ago, so I don't think she's stranded."

"She didn't mention me?"

He shook his head. "But that isn't surprising. Her mind doesn't run toward the female of the species."

"I wondered if you'd noticed," she countered before she could stop herself.

"I think you're returning to normal." His glance was sardonic as it raked over her, but he put a hand under her elbow and increased the pace. "Getting back to Angela—for a moment—"

"That's a blessing. . . ."

He ignored her murmur. "She wouldn't be caught by an out-of-place signpost in here. Rudy says she knows the place backward and forward. I could never figure out why."

Despite her discomfort, Carrie started to laugh.

He frowned down at her. "I suppose you do?" Then he was distracted by the flicker of light through the trees up ahead and said, "That's the entrance gate. We can discuss this after we get you some coffee and warm clothes."

"I'll have to sneak in the back entrance of the inn, looking like this. . . ."

"You're not going to the inn. My sister's house is a lot closer," he said as they cut across to the preserve gateway. "You can be refurbished there."

Carrie hardly heard him; she was so thankful to see the familiar surroundings that it was a moment before she could say, "You brought the station wagon," in a surprised tone.

"Well, you didn't think I was going to send you off into the night on that damned bicycle, did you?"

"I don't know." She looked around. "Where is it?"

"Where's what?"

"The bicycle." Carrie was so tired that it seemed important.

"I shoved it in the back of the wagon when I got here. It was a good thing you parked it by the gate. Otherwise I wouldn't have bothered to even start looking around here. Now, hop in the car and relax. I don't want to hear any more out of you until you're awash with hot coffee. And if you don't like the taste of my coffee, you can always pour it over your feet. It must be good for something." The last comment came as he turned on the ignition.

Carrie managed a small smile, but that was all. By then, reaction to the last few hours was setting in with a vengeance. It was difficult to keep from shaking with the cold, even though Mark had immediately switched on the car heater. She tried to relax under its warmth but found that her tense muscles wouldn't respond.

Mark was evidently watching her from the corner of his eye as they drove down the winding entrance road. "I wish I'd remembered to throw a blanket in the back. I don't know what in the hell I was thinking of."

"It's all right. The heater's starting to penetrate." She bent over and slipped off her wet shoes.

"Another five minutes and we'll be at the house," he promised, braking to a quick stop at the arterial and then accelerating in a way that made her glance at him in surprise. "Sorry," he apologized. "I don't usually drive like this. As a matter of fact, I seem to be doing a lot of strange things these days."

"I *had* noticed," Carrie said tartly.

"You must be feeling better. It takes energy to start fighting back."

"Just wait until I get warm . . ." she threatened.

"That won't be long." He nodded toward a development of houses ahead of them. "We're almost home free."

She stared through the windshield at the houses he'd indicated.

"The lights are on at your sister's house. . . ." Her voice was panicky. "I can't face anyone looking like this."

"Relax—there's nobody around. I just left in a hurry. The woman who cleans only comes in the mornings." He slowed to pull in the driveway and turned off the ignition after he'd braked. "Stay there for a minute," he instructed, getting out and slamming his door.

He moved across the tiny rectangle of lawn and then onto a porch. Carrie saw him unlock the front door and swing it wide. Then he was striding back to the car and opening her door. "Slide over here," he instructed, reaching down to lift her against his chest. "Close the car door, will you? I'm fresh out of hands."

She managed that with her left hand, even as she was saying, "You don't have to carry me. I can walk."

"Not in stocking feet." He sounded as if he carried women into his sister's house every night of the week. Carrie subsided but bit her lip as they reached the lighted porch, hoping that the neighbors weren't looking.

Mark carried her across the threshold and through a slate entranceway before depositing her on the first step of a carpeted stairway. He went back to slam the door and then brushed past her on the stairs. "C'mon up," he instructed, leading the way.

Carrie had only a moment to notice an attractive living room done in shades of green with white accents before she was following him up the carpeted treads.

He had gone into a tiled bathroom and was already turning on the hot-water tap in the tub when she caught up with him. "There's a bedroom through there," he said, indicating a second door. "Go and take off your clothes. You'll find a closet full of stuff to put on later. My sister leaves plenty of gear around."

"I can't wear her things. . . ."

His chin took on a familiar angle. "Don't be more of a damned fool than necessary."

"I suppose you'd stuff me in the bathtub, too. . . ."

"Exactly. All part of southern hospitality."

"Never mind." She started toward the bedroom. "I can manage very nicely on my own. Now that you've turned on the water, suppose you direct your talents to a coffeepot. Downstairs," she added pointedly over her shoulder.

Twenty minutes later she made her way down the stairs and followed the aroma of coffee until it led her to a small paneled study where Mark was depositing a loaded tray on a table in front of a leather davenport. A few feet away, a blaze burned in a tile-fronted fireplace.

Mark straightened to survey her. "You look considerably improved."

"I should hope so." She pirouetted slowly. "This just shows what a pound of gardenia bath salts, hot water, and some dry clothes can do. I may never give this outfit back to your sister," she added, looking approvingly down at the red tartan slacks and fisherman knit turtleneck she had borrowed. For her feet she'd found some after-ski slippers that were warm and comfortable.

Mark merely grinned and motioned her toward the davenport.

Carrie moved forward obediently. "Actually, the slacks are a little snug . . . I'm not sure I can sit down without a catastrophe."

"After what's happened tonight—that wouldn't even rate a raised eyebrow." He sat down and started to pour the coffee. "You can just back out of the room."

"Like an audience with royalty." She smiled and took the coffee from him, managing to sit down without any problems.

His grin widened. "Promises . . . promises. Ah, well, how about a sandwich? If I leave the platter in the middle, we can both help ourselves," he added, doing just that.

"Ummm." Carrie gazed at the appetizing array and then selected a thick roast-beef one. She leaned back after taking a bite and chewed slowly. "I didn't know anything could taste so good. After this I'm not leaving the inn without carrying a box lunch."

"I'm glad your appetite's come back. . . ."

"It never left. That was the trouble." She reached over and selected a dill pickle. "Now that I'm practically back to normal, you can start telling me all the things you kept under wraps when we had lunch at the fort."

His eyebrows drew together. Then he put down his sandwich on a plate and deliberately took a sip of coffee. "About Rudy, you mean?" he asked finally. "I wondered when you'd tumble." He saw the barely concealed annoyance on her delicate features, and his eyes kindled. "You can read me off another time when you have your strength back. Besides," he said, shoving the sandwiches closer, "there's no proof that Rudy's connected with this latest development."

"You still could have told me about him," she insisted.

"I thought you were in less danger the way things were, and there was a chance that he wouldn't pursue the acquaintance." His eyebrows drew together again. "Why in the hell didn't you go stay in Savannah with Roberta?"

"It wasn't your fault that I didn't. The only

thing you forgot to bring along to our tender fare-well scene was a baseball bat," she said, not meeting his glance. "You were brutal."

"I meant to be. If I'd told you the truth, would you have gone quietly?"

She carefully inspected her sandwich. "The truth about what?"

"You don't miss a thing, do you?" He grimaced. "All right, let's take Angela...." The corners of his mouth curved in the silence that followed. "Sorry."

"A Freudian slip," she murmured.

"You can drop that," he told her definitely. "Angela was simply an egg for an omelet in this thing."

"That's good—because she's decided you're not her type, either. She's smitten with a visiting lawyer named Jason Wright. I saw them together in Savannah yesterday."

"Oh?" Mark rubbed the side of his jaw. "Does Rudy know about that?"

"Apparently not. She was careful to explain when we were taking that miserable walk." Carrie's voice rose. "Do you think she ditched me because of that?" Then, before he could answer: "But that's ridiculous. I told her I wouldn't say anything, so there can't be any connection."

"I think you're right. Or if she did waylay you, it was just a warning to stay out of her love life. Believe me, if Rudy had any suspicions, he would have used a different set of rules entirely," he said in a somber tone. "That's why I couldn't take a chance on your being involved with me."

"You were certainly cagey. It wasn't until Roberta explained about Jason Wright defending an electronics manufacturer yesterday that I started wondering. Then, when I was sitting on that miserable stump, I began to think about Angela's part in the scheme."

"I don't believe there's any connection. She's probably just keeping her Jason under wraps. . . ."

"Until they can make it legal?"

"That wasn't what I had in mind." His eyes took on a wicked gleam. "All right—let's give Angela the benefit of doubt, but not because of her morals. She's fresh out of them."

"You'd know better than I. . . ."

He started laughing. "And we were doing so well, too. Would it help to mention that that was an editorial comment?"

"It sounds better, but I don't know whether I believe you," Carrie said, wishing she could. She finished her last bite of sandwich and used her napkin. "Umm . . . that tasted good."

"More coffee?"

"No, thanks." When she stretched her legs toward the fireplace, she found that it was an effort to keep from yawning. For an instant she let herself dwell on how nice it would be to share this house with him for more than an hour or so. Or, being entirely truthful, to share . . . more than the house. She kept her thick lashes partially lowered as her gaze lingered on Mark's profile. It was carefully expressionless; if he were feeling any pangs of desire, they were well hidden. His next words proved they were completely nonexistent.

"I'd better get you back to the inn," he said briskly, rising to his feet and pulling the screen across the front of the fireplace. "You need a good night's sleep."

"I'm ready whenever you are. It's a shame to drag you out again—you look as if you could use some sleep, too." She ignored his sudden scowl as she headed for the stairs. "Could I borrow a plastic bag or something for my clothes?"

"Leave them. I'll get them dry and return them later." He took a poplin jacket from a hook on the closet door and handed it to her. "Wear this over your sweater. There's no sense in getting chilled again."

Carrie accepted it without comment. As she shoved her arms into the jacket sleeves, she decided that it simply wasn't her night. Mark had evidently cataloged her in the "invalid" category, and she didn't have the strength or the time to change his mind.

She guided their conversation accordingly on the drive back to the inn. There was nothing discussed that didn't have to do with wind direction, cloud cover, or what was happening to the humidity.

Therefore, Mark's movements when he braked in the inn parking lot came as a complete surprise. Carrie had just begun her carefully worded speech of thanks when he leaned across her and opened the station-wagon door. "You can skip all that," he told her tersely. "I'm going up with you and check the room."

"Surely that isn't necessary. . . ."

"Probably not, but I'm doing it anyhow." He waited until she was out of the car and then locked it after her.

Carrie's room looked sterile and austere after the warmth of Mark's house. She refrained from saying anything, merely going around turning on the lights and upping the dial on the thermostat.

Mark checked the dressing-room closet and shoved aside the shower curtain in the bathroom before emerging to inspect the lock on her balcony window.

Carrie watched with a suggestion of a twinkle in her eye. When he moved toward the door, she let out an audible sigh.

Mark turned instantly. "What's the matter?"

"I was waiting for you to look under the bed. All my life, I've wanted to see somebody do that. You're a terrible disappointment."

The set expression on his face softened. "And you're a lousy liar. There isn't room for a thin pygmy under all that," he said, jerking his head toward the wide bed, "let alone our friend Forza."

"Was *that* who you were looking for? Rudy wouldn't hang around waiting—he'd simply come calling later."

Mark leveled a finger. "Well, let me tell you this. If *anybody* comes calling later tonight—and I don't give a damn who it is—you don't answer, and you certainly don't open the door. Understand?"

His serious tone wiped away all levity from her face. "Yes, of course. But I can't stay sealed in here forever...."

"I know that. We have every reason to think Rudy'll be moving the parts tonight or tomorrow."

"You're keeping watch? I didn't know..."

"You weren't meant to. We work in shifts." He frowned as he went on thoughtfully, "I'll be busy most of tomorrow. It would be better if you were safely off the island. You could go into Savannah...."

"There's no need for that," Carrie told him. "I'll be careful." She moved with him toward the door.

"I don't want you hanging around here alone tomorrow," he insisted. "If you won't be sensible, then you'd better come down and stay on the boat with me. Bring a lunch along. If Rudy comes visiting, he can think what he likes."

"Knowing Rudy, he'll put two and two together and realize we were together the other morning."

"He probably has already. Besides, my relationship with Angela has outlived its usefulness. Rudy undoubtedly knows all about Jason Wright."

"I think Angela has kept some of the juicier details off-the-record," Carrie said with a tired smile.

Her pale face seemed to remind Mark that he'd returned her to the inn for sleep, not conversation.

He nodded briskly. "Okay, then, I'll see you tomorrow. You can take your time—Rudy never makes any moves before noon—he's part night owl. So if there's no break later tonight, we might as well both sleep late."

"All right. Thanks again." Carrie tried to sound casual as the sudden silence between them became an awkward chasm and Mark still hesitated by the door. Surely he wasn't going to shake hands. Uneasily, she brushed a strand of hair from her cheek.

That tremulous gesture broke the spell.

"Oh, the hell with it!" Mark said violently, and reached out to pull her against him with such force that it took her breath away. "So much for good intentions," he muttered as he bent his head and kissed her.

The kiss ended just as abruptly as it began. A minute later he had thrust her away from him and was commanding with a thick voice, "Lock this damned door after me. Do you hear?"

He saw her nod dazedly, and brought his palm up for an instant to caress her cheek—as if he had to touch her just once more. Then he was gone.

Chapter Eight

Even the distinct sound of raindrops hitting her balcony window couldn't faze Carrie's high spirits when she awoke the next morning. The hours that had passed since Mark's departure hadn't dimmed her certainty that his behavior wasn't that of a man who planned never to see a woman again. As she lay in bed thinking about that hard, seeking kiss that he'd bestowed, she took a deep breath and stretched ecstatically. Then she shoved aside the covers and went over to the window. She stared thoughtfully at the rain gusts blowing across the beach, while noting the gray swells on the ocean's surface, and felt the first nigglings of unease.

The prospect of spending the day aboard a bobbing cabin cruiser in the middle of the sound—even in the company of the only man in the world—made her stomach muscles tighten apprehensively.

As she dressed in a pair of camel-and-blue-checked slacks topped with a camel cashmere sweater, she decided that Mark's plans might have changed overnight. That cheerful prospect made her choose scrambled eggs for breakfast rather than the "tea-and-toast" menu she'd decided was prudent for a day afloat.

The inn waitress was glad to take her order for a picnic lunch and promised to have it ready a little later.

When Carrie returned to her room for her coat after breakfast, the weather hadn't improved. The intermittent squalls had settled into a permanent gray umbrella over the island, and rain was beating against the window in a steady downpour. Carrie spared a moment to be grateful that she wasn't still sitting out in the middle of the forest preserve experiencing nature at first hand. She shuddered even at the thought, and shrugged into a blue trench coat guaranteed to keep out the elements.

She was leaving her room when the box containing the stuffed hippo caught her eye. Her eyes gleamed with laughter, and she went back to tuck it under her arm. Mark might as well be custodian until it could be delivered to his niece.

The box was so large that it rated a special trip to the car, and then Carrie made another trip to stow away the lunch basket, protected from the rain by its wicker cover.

The blasts of wind buffeted her light car as she drove south toward the marina, and she turned the dial on the radio to try and find a weather report. Just as she reached the parking lot next to the harbor, she heard the last of a newscast advising that gale warnings had been posted along the coast, and small-craft warnings for inland waters.

It didn't take a weather forecast to determine that, Carrie decided with a worried look at the flag by the marina. The ensign was stretched to full length and snapping in the wind. Carrie's glance went beyond it and the rows of moored boats to note the scudding whitecaps frosting the green waters of the sound. She thought of the seasick pill she'd taken before leaving the inn and then patted her raincoat pocket to make sure that she'd brought reinforcements.

Mark must have been watching for her, because she had only gotten halfway down the pier when he stepped from the stern of the cruiser and came hurrying to meet her.

"No one could accuse you of traveling light," he said, reaching over to take the lunch basket and then appropriating the gift box with some difficulty. "What in the Sam Hill is all this?"

"It's a long story." She noted his waterproof jacket and denims as she fell into step beside him. Obviously they were still destined for a day afloat. She took a deep breath and let it out slowly.

He must have been watching. "What's the matter? Don't you feel well?" Strangely enough, he sounded ill-at-ease, as if he was unsure of her mood after their parting the night before.

That uncharacteristic reaction suddenly made her spirits rise. She pulled up as they reached the stern of the cruiser and waited for him to go aboard first. "I feel fine . . . now," she said, smiling. "A minute ago, I was going to suggest having lunch in the parking lot."

"Oh, that!" He grinned back at her. "It's all in your mind. Use positive thought, and you'll forget about your stomach. Besides, today you can take the wheel up on the flying bridge if you start feeling queasy." He disappeared into the cabin to deposit the lunch and the box, but was back a moment later to help her aboard.

She accepted his hand gratefully for the transfer to the cruiser's bobbing deck and steadied herself against the sliding glass door to the cabin. "I gather you're on the dawn patrol. Wasn't there any action at the Forza house last night?"

He shook his head. "Nobody left the place all night long. The only flurry of activity came this morning when a crew of gardeners arrived. I have a feeling in my bones that good old Rudy is laughing his head off at our efforts."

"The way Angela must have laughed when she left me on the nature walk," Carrie admitted ruefully. "I'm glad that you invited me to the final act."

"Hey . . . not so fast. I don't know that there's going to be a final act today. Even if we luck it in, it'll be no place for a woman." As he saw her chin tilt challengingly, he added, "There's no use arguing with me. The Coast Guard and the IRS men will be in charge if Rudy tries to take his merchandise out of our waters."

"But you'll be there, won't you?"

"Depends where he makes the break." He motioned her in to the cabin and then moved over to switch on the blower.

Carrie's glance followed him. "Are we going somewhere?"

"Uh-huh. There's nothing to be gained hanging around here. Make yourself comfortable—we'll be under way in a few minutes."

"I gathered that." Carrie's feminine pride was fraying at the edges, and it showed in her voice. She hadn't expected Mark to fall at her feet and murmur sweet nothings, but it seemed reasonable to expect some indication of affection. Apparently his nervousness had stemmed from a fear that she'd fall all over him after one good-night kiss.

Mark was staring at her with a narrowed glance. "Exactly what are you hatching now?" he asked ominously.

Carrie's eyes widened.

"And don't give me that stricken-ingenue bit," he continued. "Are you going to follow orders today, or will I have trouble again?"

She thought it over. "I *could* take my lunch and go home," she pointed out after some hesitation.

"You could." He tried to keep his voice solemn, although an undercurrent of amusement crept in. "But I hope you won't."

"You're hungry . . ."

"That, too."

"Well, at least you could tell me where we're going." It wasn't an official surrender, but Carrie knew that it might as well be.

Mark's fleeting expression of triumph showed he recognized it, too. "Probably back to the shrimp-boat dock." His attention was distracted by a man carrying some fishing gear who was walking across the end of the dock toward the parking lot. "There might have been a change of plan," Mark said. "I'd better go see. Stay here and keep out of sight . . . I'll be right back."

He was gone swiftly up the pier toward the marina before Carrie could reply. She watched him with a slight frown and then turned back to the cabin.

To keep occupied, she unpacked the lunch basket and stowed the perishables into the compact refrigerator in the cruiser's galley. Afterward she checked the coffeepot on top of the stove and discovered that it only needed reheating. Before she could go further, she heard footsteps, and the cabin floor listed suddenly. Carrie peered through the galley porthole and saw Mark loosen their stern line and then move rapidly to cast off at the bow. An instant later he was back in the cabin and standing by the instrument panel flicking on the ignition switch.

He acknowledged Carrie's presence only after they had pulled away from the mooring and the cruiser's bow was pointed toward the middle of the sound. "There's a bottle of motion pills on the shelf in the forward cabin," he said. "You'd better take one. The wind's kicking up."

"I can tell." She braced herself against the counter. "It's all right; I took one before I came aboard. Are we still going to the shrimp-boat dock?"

He nodded, keeping his attention on the throttles until they were adjusted to his satisfaction. Then he braced himself against the bench by the panel and half-turned to face her. "Sorry about the rush, but I just got word that Angela and her boyfriend stopped by the house and are now on the road to the marina. There's nothing to be gained by letting her see you with me."

Carrie felt a surge of disappointment. "Then nothing important's happened?"

"You mean Rudy?" Mark looked weary as he shook his head. "Maybe he's decided to hole up for the winter like the alligators. Is there any coffee left?"

"Uh-huh. I was just going to reheat it." She turned on the stove burner and said over her shoulder, "Do I have to work my passage on this trip?"

"Absolutely. You can't expect the run of the ship without a little honest toil."

By the time the coffee was hot, he was altering their course and checking to see if any other pleasure craft had left the island marina. Only after he'd finished did he reach out absently to take the coffee mug she was holding. "Thanks. Are you having some?"

She nodded and went back to the galley to raise her own mug in a mock salute. Then, after the first swallow, she shuddered and poured the contents down the sink drain. "I don't mind reheated coffee, but that tastes as if it's been reconstructed. When did you make it, for heaven's sake?"

"Sometime after midnight." He didn't protest as she took his mug and emptied it down the sink as well, but he commented, "I'll need something to stay awake for the rest of the day. Better make some fresh."

As he turned his attention to the approaching shrimp-boat dock, Carrie had an opportunity to note the lines of weariness that etched his eyes and mouth. From the way he talked, he'd had practically no sleep after he'd left her. Even as she watched, he yawned and put up a hand to massage the muscles at the back of his neck.

Carrie's lips curved gently in sympathy. The man was practically out on his feet. All the time she'd been wondering why he was being so casual about her presence, he was barely managing to stay awake. "Did you have any breakfast?" she asked finally.

"Not officially. There were some crackers left, but the cupboard's getting bare." He spun the wheel gently and slackened off on their speed. "We can replenish it at the grocery here," he added, nodding toward the wooden pier ahead of them on the right. "Can you put down the fenders on that side to keep us off the pilings?"

"Just dump them over the edge?"

"That's all." He gave her a worried glance as she slid open the cabin door. "Be careful and hang on. I'd rather lose some paint than you."

Which wasn't exactly a comment for a balcony

scene, but Carrie hugged every last syllable to her breast as she made her way on deck and clung to the bow rail as she lowered the rubber fenders. The white froth on the choppy waves dissolved to spindrift in the troughs, and the cruiser wallowed as Mark cut their power. Carrie flattened herself against the grab rail as he moved quickly out of the cabin and secured the stern line.

"I can get the bow," she told him as he turned toward her.

"Wait until I bring it closer," he instructed, disappearing back into the cabin. A moment later a powerful surge of the engine brought the pier bollard within easy reach, and Carrie looped the line around it, trying to copy Mark's move at the stern.

"Good girl." He was beside her before she was half through, and finished securing it. Then he surveyed the creaking dock above them and laughed. "I hope it lasts the day."

"It must have been here since the carpetbaggers. So much for solid land."

Mark caught up with her as she went back in the comfortable warm cabin. "Is the motion bothering you?"

Carrie glanced up at him, surprised. "Do you know, I'd forgotten about it until just now. I must have gotten my sea legs or something."

"Good." He folded his long length onto a padded bench and picked up a pair of binoculars. "That's one good thing."

She frowned. "Why? What would you have done otherwise?"

"Sent you back to the inn." He had the glasses at his eyes, and he was training them on Hilton Head across the water. "There's a telephone up at the grocery store, and there must be some kind of cab service around here."

"Thanks a lot."

He kept the glasses in position. "Can't see anything happening over there. Angela must have decided not to take the boat out—so there's still hope that Rudy will come aboard later." He put the binoculars on a ledge within easy reach. "What did you say a minute ago?"

Carrie was already regretting her impulsive comment. "Nothing important. What's next?"

"Lunch, I hope." He stood up and stretched. "After that, I'll go up and call to find out what's happening."

Carrie trailed behind him toward the galley. "There's a radio aboard, isn't there?"

"Sure." He was bending over the refrigerator, surveying its contents.

"Well?"

"Well, what?"

"Why not use it? Instead of a pay telephone a block away?"

He straightened and put out a hand to ruffle her hair. "Use your head, woman. The ship-to-shore's a great big party line."

"But in an emergency . . ."

"Then we've made other arrangements. Right

179

now, I want information—but not as much as I want one of those." He was investigating a neatly wrapped tuna-fish sandwich.

Carrie stacked the rest of them on a plate that she'd taken from the cupboard. "James Bond wouldn't have been sidetracked by food."

"As I remember, he was sidetracked by quite a few other things, but you're too young to know about that. Shall I carry that stuff to the table?"

"If you make sure there's a sandwich left for me when it gets there," she stipulated. "That's my commission. Here's a thermos of coffee, too."

He took it in his other hand. "Did I ever mention what sterling qualities you possess?"

"Never," she said firmly.

"That's too bad. Shakespeare had a name for women like you, but I'm too hungry to remember," he said, putting the plate down and pulling a folding table from a storage cabinet. "Do we need any silver?"

"I don't think so." Carrie ran her eye over the provisions and then gathered some napkins in one hand and coffee mugs in the other. "This should take care of everything."

She noticed that he arranged the table where it was convenient to keep an eye on the South Island marina breakwater.

"Who takes the first shift?" she asked, settling on the bench beside him and reaching to pour from the thermos.

"First shift for what?"

She took a patient breath. "Look, among those

sterling qualities you've ignored is a fair-to-middling brain. I can see a boat across the water just as well as you can, and there's no sense in both of us ending up with indigestion."

His slow smile appeared. "That makes sense. Suppose you eat your lunch in peace and then man the binoculars while I go up and phone. It's going to be a long afternoon."

Carrie nodded and settled back comfortably on the bench herself after that. Lunch was an amicable meal, and she was happy to see that Mark looked considerably better after he had worked his way through sandwiches and salad.

"Dessert's on the thin side," Carrie announced, checking the picnic basket and bringing out another plastic-wrapped plate. "We only have cookies to go with the last cup of coffee. I don't know what kind they are. . . ."

Mark craned forward to investigate. "That shows your northern upbringing, my girl. Any southerner would recognize those at twenty paces." He reached over and helped himself while she folded the wrapping and put it back in the basket. "Maybe they'll be an omen—lord knows, we could use one."

"You've lost me. They look like sugar cookies with some kind of seed on them—sesame, I think." She took an exploratory nibble. "And they taste good."

"You're right about that." Mark reached for another one. "But it's not sesame in this part of the world—that's benne seed when you're south of the

Mason-Dixon line. The slaves are reported to have brought it with them from Africa."

"I had no idea." Carrie peered at the cookie plate with renewed interest. "But what's this about an omen?"

"Depends on how superstitious you are. In some parts, benne seeds count for good luck. No self-respecting kitchen should be without them."

"And much tidier than a rabbit's foot," she said. "But how about a small hippo?"

"A what?"

"Never mind," she said hastily, deciding that this wasn't the time. "I'll tell you later. If I'd only known, I could have brought along my voodoo doll from home."

"The theory being that if we used enough pins, Rudy would get out of town?"

"With a pain in his side or something like that." She pursed her lips. "I suppose it would be too much to hope that he'd set sail for international waters."

" 'Fraid so, especially when he isn't even aboard his boat." Mark took a last swallow of coffee and hauled himself erect. "I'd better go check in. Don't bother clearing this stuff away—I'll do it when I come back."

"It won't take a minute." Carrie cradled her coffee mug between her palms and peered through the glass of the cabin. "You'd better put on some foul-weather gear. The rain's started again."

"Damn!" Mark bent down to follow her glance. "It's a pity we couldn't go south for the winter."

Carrie started to laugh. "I thought I had."

"Farther south, then. This looks as if it's settling in for the rest of the year." He went down the steps to the forward cabin, emerging a minute later with a nylon windbreaker. "If the wind keeps blowing, at least we won't have to worry about fog."

"You sound like a man who's trying to find something cheerful and is having a hard time."

"Not as hard now as fifteen minutes ago," he confessed, shrugging into the jacket. "You supply a very nice lunch—I'll have to shanghai you more often."

She glanced demurely up at him from the corner of her eye. "I think the original word was 'abduct.'"

"That's ancient history, and you know it. Keep an eye on the marina while I'm gone, will you?" A fast-breaking wave made him clutch the grab rail, and he turned to add, "Don't move around any more than you have to, and stay inside. I'll check our moorage."

Carrie found it no trouble at all to simply nod agreement to all those orders. Mark's comments made sense; she found it difficult to even walk around the galley putting the food away, and later carefully erected chrome sea rails around the pot on the stove when she made fresh coffee. When it was safely started, she rummaged in her purse and found another pill for motion sickness. "Better safe than sorry," she murmured to herself, washing it down with the last swallow of thermos coffee.

She had no intention of hanging over the stern rail on this trip; once was enough.

She went back to the cabin and picked up Mark's binoculars. A quick look across the turbulent waters of the sound showed there was nothing new, and she turned to use them on the length of the shrimp-boat pier.

Mark had disappeared around the corner of the net house, which was so old and flimsy-looking that Carrie wondered how many more windstorms it could survive. Like the wooden pier beside the cruiser, it must be sturdier than it looked.

Even as she lowered the glasses, another gust of wind made the nearby oaks and palmettos give way and slammed shut a door at the end of the net shed. Moments later, in the lull that followed, the door creaked open again like something in a haunted house.

An involuntary shiver coursed through Carrie, and she closed a glass panel designed for ventilation. The warm, comfortable cabin seemed safer without a reminder of the outside world. She glanced across the threatening gray water between their moorage and Hilton Head. It wasn't a day for cruising in small pleasure craft as far as she was concerned, but she wasn't going to mention it to Mark. Despite his affable manner, she knew that he had every intention of putting her ashore if anything interesting happened. Whether or not he succeeded depended on how long she could keep him away from the Hilton Head marina.

Her gaze raked the deserted and rain-swept pier

beside the cruiser, and she smiled in faint triumph. At least she didn't have to worry about being abandoned in such a dreary spot. Even Mark wouldn't be that heartless.

She was calmly pouring herself a cup of fresh coffee when she felt his weight on deck, and without hesitating, reached for another cup.

He paused on the stern transom long enough to slip out of his soaking windbreaker, and then slipped inside, with it bundled in his hand. "Back in a minute," he said, striding through the cabin and trying to keep the water from the carpet. "I'll hang this in the shower to dry off."

She followed and watched him arrange it on a hanger. "There's nothing going on across the way—at least, not that I could see. Did you hear anything new?"

"Just a description of Angela's heartthrob."

"Big deal," she scoffed. "I could have saved you a walk in the rain. I had plenty of time to admire her chum in Savannah."

"Ummm. Well, today she's using his muscles to carry groceries aboard. Looks as if they're getting ready for a big celebration."

"That fits. Although I didn't get the idea they were going to use Rudy's cruiser for transportation." She frowned as she tried to remember.

"Maybe they didn't know." Mark was intent on blotting his wet hair with the towel. Afterward he tossed the damp linen back on a rack and used his comb briefly. "There's nothing strange about partying aboard that cruiser. Rudy's outfitted it with all the luxuries."

Carrie wrinkled her nose at his voice of experience. "Too bad Angela's found new fish to fry. . . ."

"*Isn't* it," he agreed cordially. "But as long as we're on the subject of food—is that fresh coffee for me?"

She nodded, not having completely forgiven him for the way he'd changed the subject. Apparently his past dates with Angela were not open for discussion. Frowning, she watched him take a swallow. "Did anyone ever tell you that you have a preoccupation with food?"

His eyebrows climbed in appreciation of her remark. "What brought that on?"

"Every time we get together, we're eating something. I was thinking about it while you were making your phone call." She was aware that he was having a hard time keeping a straight face, but she continued stubbornly, "I mean it—we've drunk coffee from dawn to midnight, on land and on sea. . . ."

"With the rocket's red glare . . ." He broke off as her frown deepened. "Sorry, wrong verse."

"I'm serious," she informed him. "There are other things besides food."

"I'm well aware of them." He went on conversationally, "You'd think that being half-dead for sleep would have helped me when you're around, but it doesn't do a damned thing. And if we don't change the subject pretty soon, or if you don't go to the other end of the cabin and sit down and behave yourself"—he watched in some amusement as the color flared under her cheekbones—"then I'm going to have to take *another* walk along the pier. Do I make myself clear?"

Carrie had to swallow before she found her voice. "Perfectly, thanks. What do you want me to do?"

"There's no point in doubling up on our watch. If you can hold the fort here for another hour, I could catch a nap in the forward cabin," he went on in a carefully expressionless tone. "Wake me if you see anything that even looks like Rudy's cruiser leaving the marina. Okay?"

"Yes, of course." She watched him move to the instrument panel and flip a switch. "What are you doing now?"

"This is ship-to-shore—an emergency channel. If you hear a transmission on it, give me a shout. Don't touch anything," he warned as she peered around him.

"I wasn't going to." Carrie wrinkled her nose. "Remind me to deliver my equal-rights lecture sometime. Usually I save it for our baritones, but . . ."

"I fit right in." His eyes sparked wickedly. "It's kind of you to take an interest. We'll have to pursue it . . ."

"At another time," she said, moving prudently out of reach. "Go take your nap."

He yawned enormously. "While you meditate on my sins. But don't forget to keep your eyes on that marina breakwater in the meantime."

After Mark disappeared into the forward cabin and partially closed the folding door, Carrie obediently resumed her perch, with the binoculars close at hand.

In all the time that followed, the marine traffic emerging from the island marina consisted solely of a small work boat and a slightly larger shrimp trawler that apparently detoured in for emergency provisions. Since the storm didn't lessen as the afternoon wore on, Carrie wasn't surprised that the pleasure craft stayed snugly in their berths. Apparently Angela and Jason Wright must have decided that getting away from it all—even to the more sheltered waters of the inside passage—should be postponed for better weather. A flaming love affair would be hard to maintain when the participants had to keep a grip on the furniture as well as each other. So much for love afloat, Carrie decided, wishing she could improve the script.

She glanced at her watch and frowned. Mark had said to wake him in an hour, but she'd decided to let him sleep on. By now he'd slept almost two and a half hours; probably he'd be annoyed if she waited any longer.

Even as she got to her feet, the vinyl door of the forward cabin was shoved forcibly aside and Mark's tall figure appeared. His hair was rumpled, and there was no disguising that he'd slept in his clothes. There was also no disguising the fact that he was madder than hell.

"For god's sake, Carrie, don't you know what time it is!" he snarled as he reached in the bathroom and snaked his jacket out. "I said to wake me in an hour!"

"But you needed the sleep . . ." He muttered something savage that Carrie didn't even try to translate, and she pressed on, "Besides, nothing's happened. I've watched every minute, so I don't see why you're so mad. . . ."

"Because I'm supposed to check in . . . that's why, damnit."

"But they could have reached you on the radio. . . ."

He was zipping his jacket and pulling aside the glass cabin door even as he growled, "Thanks. I'll tell them that you said so."

She wilted visibly. "Mark . . . I'm sorry. I didn't think . . ."

"And I have a hell of a temper," he said, his expression softening, "but that's no reason to take my responsibility out on you. I'll be back."

When he did return five minutes later, Carrie's attention was trained on a sleek vessel that was just then emerging from the breakwater at Hilton Head. "Look, Mark, they're getting under way. That's Rudy's boat, isn't it?" Her voice rose with excitement.

"Looks like it," he said calmly.

Her glance widened. "But don't you even care? I thought that's what you were waiting for."

"We were waiting for Rudy to make a move. Not his oversexed little sister and her tall, dark boyfriend, who've decided to tie up overnight at one of the islands nearby. It may be their idea of fun, but it's another damned day wasted as far as we're concerned. Rudy hasn't stuck his nose out of their house."

"You mean you won't even follow the cruiser?"

"There's a chopper to make sure they're not headed out to sea. The patrol boat will make a routine check on their anchorage later. It isn't Angela we want!" He stared at Carrie's profile. "What's the matter? Is this weather getting to you?"

"No, that isn't it." She pressed her fingers harder against her forehead, trying to think. "Something isn't right," she told him. "Who did you say was with Angela?"

"Some good-looking crewman from the ship. He's been along before when Rudy's taken the cruiser out. Apparently today he's making time without a chaperon."

"Good-looking? You're sure?"

Mark's eyes narrowed. "That's what they said. I know the man they're talking about. Six feet or thereabouts. Straight dark hair—not as good a profile as Rudy's, but not bad."

"That's not Jason Wright," Carrie said positively.

"I didn't say it was." Mark was staring at her.

"Yes, but it *should* be—don't you see? That afternoon in Savannah, Angela and Jason Wright were planning an elopement . . . or to go away together. And they were going today—he'd even arranged passports and all that."

"But what makes you so sure anything's changed?"

"Because Jason Wright is sort of overweight and looks as if he stepped out of a Prussian novel extolling the virtues of the Aryan race. There hasn't been a brunette in his family tree for two generations. Are you sure you got the story right?"

Mark nodded slowly. "They reported Angela arrived at the dock clutching this guy as if she wanted him wrapped for Christmas. And there's no missing Angela—all long hair, sunglasses, and floppy hat. I've seen that get-up of hers. She looks like a fugitive from a Hollywood supermarket."

There was a moment's silence as Carrie stared up at him. Then she said flatly, "I just don't believe it. Not after what I saw. And there was no fudging on that, because they didn't know I was there."

"Then you think this is out of character for Angela?"

"Absolutely." She paused to consider. "Unless she's playing a part for Rudy."

"But why would he want her aboard?"

"I don't know." Carrie gestured toward the island breakwater as the Forza Down Easter turned into the waters of the sound and proceeded steadily north. "If Rudy were aboard, your people wouldn't be watching him sail off into the sunset with just a routine check later on."

"What are you getting at?" Mark's tone was sharp.

Carrie gripped her hands together so tightly that her nails cut into her palms. "If I wanted to play games, I'd get a black wig, a floppy hat, and some sunglasses. They're Angela's trademark—so nobody gives them a second look."

Mark was moving over to the instrument panel to throw a switch for the bilge motor even before she'd finished speaking. "That's the damnedest reasoning I've heard, but we can't afford to leave anything to chance."

"Are we going to follow the cruiser by ourselves or get some more help?" Carrie asked in a voice tense with anticipation.

"I'm not sure." Mark pulled a piece of paper from his shirt pocket and rummaged alongside the radio until he found a pencil. He wrote down a number and thrust it at her. "Here! You'll have to phone for instructions. Wait a minute . . ." His voice caught her as she started toward the stern. "Go and put a sweater under your raincoat. But hurry up, will you."

Breathlessly she did as he asked. "What shall I tell them on the phone?"

"Just what you've told me. . . ."

"Damn!" She fumbled with a stubborn buttonhole. "Now I'm ready. No . . . I don't have any change. . . ." She turned and tried to remember where she'd put her purse.

"For god's sake . . . take this." Mark shoved some coins into her hand and pushed her toward the stern. "I'll help you up on the dock."

"All right." She huddled away from the pelting

rain as they got out from under cover. "I can help cast off when I come back. I'll be as quick as I can," she added, tightening her hood as the water ran down her cheeks. "What a stinking day!"

"I know." His hands reached for her waist as he bent to boost her onto the ancient wooden planking of the dock. "Carrie . . ." As she glanced questioningly at him, he cleared his throat and went on, "Be careful—stay under cover as much as you can."

"*Now* you tell me that the telephone booth leaks." Then she gasped as he swung her up, and a moment later found herself scrabbling on all fours on the pier. She got to her feet, brushing her dirty palms against her raincoat even as she saw Mark disappear back into the cruiser.

Her fingers tightened on the slip of paper with the precious phone number, and she set off, crouching over to avoid the downpour as a new gust swept along the dock. When she reached the corner of the net warehouse, she paused an instant to get her bearings and glanced automatically back to their mooring.

"Oh, no!" Her anguished exclamation was lost as the warehouse door next to her creaked on its sagging hinges. But even if she'd shouted to the heavens, she couldn't have changed the scene that met her eyes.

While she watched, the stretch of open water between the cruiser and the pier widened from three to six feet. She saw Mark's figure on deck, moving swiftly to pull up the fenders. The bow and stern lines were already thrown hastily clear.

"Mark . . . wait! Wait for me!" She started running and was halfway back to the end of the dock, trying to keep her balance on the slippery planks, when she heard his shout.

"Go back, Carrie. I'll send someone. As soon as I can. . . ."

She pulled up to shriek a protest, but her words were cut off by the sudden rumble of the cruiser's engine. Simultaneously, a froth erupted from the twin screws.

An instant later, all she could see was the back of Mark's tall figure on the flying bridge as the cruiser's bow knifed through the stormy waters of the sound, heading north at full speed.

It had to be a mistake, Carrie decided frantically. Mark couldn't just go off and leave her. No man could do that deliberately—not if he cared about a woman.

But even though she stood like a rain-battered statue and watched until the boat disappeared in the cove at Skull Creek, it was plain that Mark didn't once look back.

Chapter Nine

The sun had barely made a decent arrival over Hilton Head the next morning when the phone in Carrie's room at the inn rang for the first time.

She rolled over in bed and picked up the receiver. After hearing Mark's voice say, "Carrie?" she promptly hung up. The phone rang again a minute later, and she got up to turn on the water in the shower so she could ignore it completely.

When she emerged from the bathroom ten minutes later and slipped into an apricot velour robe, she wasn't surprised that the phone had stopped ringing. Whatever the rest of Mark's faults, he wasn't slow to grasp the obvious. After his action, it was surprising that he'd even bothered to phone and apologize.

Carrie shoved her hands in the pockets of her robe, putting off packing her suitcase for just a little longer. By rights, she should have done it eight hours before, when the sheriff's deputy had finally driven her back to the inn and escorted her to her door.

He was a kindly man who tried to hide his surprise when he found Carrie huddled in a phone booth at the end of the windswept pier staring bitterly at the "Closed" sign on a tiny general store nearby.

When she left her pocket-sized shelter and went to meet him, he looked at her keenly. "Miss Shaw?" At her nod, he went on, "They said you could use a lift. Glad I arrived before it got completely dark." He jerked his head toward the deserted dock. "This is a lonely place when it storms. In weather like this, the trawlers tie up around the cove, where there's more shelter." He was opening his car door for her. "I'll put the heater on as soon as we get going."

After they were bouncing over a rutted dirt road toward the highway, he continued in friendly fashion, "I would have been here sooner, except there were some wires down by the bridge to the island, and I had to wait for the power crew. Hope you weren't worried."

"No, of course not," Carrie assured him politely. She couldn't admit that she had very little choice but to wait. There had been no taxicabs to call, and no answer when she tried the number Mark had given her.

Nor was there any answer later when she rang the number from her room at the inn. By then her curiosity was clashing with outraged feminine pride and the knowledge that she'd been treated like an utter simpleton.

Sleep was impossible in that mood; her weary body refused to relax, and her thoughts revolved like they'd been thrown into a concrete mixer. For a while she sat and stared at the picture of sea grass on the wall, and then she wandered over to her balcony to stare through the frail moonlight at the hummocks of real sea grass on the beach. But in her mind's eye, all she could see was that gap of open water when Mark had cast off and left her.

He could have explained, she kept telling herself. Or taken her along. Or transferred her to another boat. There was a long list of things he could have done, and she thought about every one of them until four o'clock in the morning, when she finally sat down on the bed and fell deeply asleep. Almost as if she'd been hit over the head with an anchor.

It wasn't surprising then that the phone call two and a half hours later did little to endear her to the caller. She was groggy, and her head ached from the tears she'd shed. When she heard Mark's voice, her partially cooled anger flared from ashes into a fiery flame.

But the phone call served one purpose; it revealed that Mark hadn't perished in the storm. At two A.M. that possibility had caused some of the tears that had caused the headache. Which was ridiculous, she'd decided under the shower. A simple drowning was too good for the creature. Now that he was back ashore, he undoubtedly planned to soothe any misgivings by a phone call. He might even invite her to lunch. Provided she brought the lunch.

When Carrie had turned off the shower faucet,

she'd given it a sharp twist, wishing she could have used the same grip on Mark's throat. The man was completely despicable, stubborn, unfeeling, utterly without redemption. Any woman fool enough to stay in his vicinity was destined to find his size-twelve shoe planted squarely on the back of her neck.

The alternative was to run—not walk—to the nearest exit, she told herself. By the time Mark got around to calling in person, he'd find his latest victim out of range.

Carrie hauled her suitcase onto the bed, thinking it was too bad that feminine pride wouldn't let her discover what happened to Rudy and Angela. The sheriff's deputy hadn't mentioned anything about boarding parties on the high seas, and under the circumstances, she could scarcely call the Forza household and ask who was around to be counted.

The buzzer at her hall door made her freeze in the middle of folding a sweater. Then, as the noise sounded again, she dropped the cardigan on the bed and moved over to the locked door. "Who is it?" she asked suspiciously.

"Maintenance man, ma'am. Your air-conditioner's overheating—they sent me to check on it."

Carrie's eyebrows drew together. "I don't think there's anything wrong with it. You must have the wrong room."

"No, ma'am. They called from downstairs."

"What's your name?" Probably the man was a

perfectly reputable employee, but Carrie wasn't in the mood to take chances.

"Ben, ma'am." His tone was patient. "I take care of all the electrical installations."

"Just a minute, please." Carrie hurried to her bedside phone and a moment later was asking for the clerk on the reception desk. "Do you have a man named Ben checking your air-conditioning?"

The woman's voice was surprised. "Why, yes, Miss Shaw. Ben Somers. He's been with us ever since the inn opened."

"And he's on duty now?"

"He should be. Is there something wrong?"

"I guess not." Carrie couldn't explain further without revealing her needless fears. "Thank you very much," she told the mystified clerk, and hung up.

Even with that official reassurance, she kept the chain on her door as she opened it and found herself facing an elderly man wearing a pair of green coveralls and carrying a metal toolbox in his hand. "I'm sorry," she said, slipping the chain free to pull the door wide. "I'm trying to get packed. If you want to make any repairs, I'll be out of the room in half an hour."

"That's okay, ma'am." He moved past her across the room to the metal air-climatizer under the wide window. "I'll check this out now and make sure that it's not getting too hot. Then I can take care of the rest later."

She watched him bend down and remove one of the metal grids. Afterward, he reached inside and

turned on the fan at high speed, then punched another control to make it idle.

"There's the trouble," he reported over his
shoulder. "Just a bad connection...." He was
rummaging in the toolbox at his side. "Wouldn't
you know..."

"What's the matter?"

"Every wrench but the one I need." He tossed
his collection back in the box with a noisy crash
and fastened the lid. "Won't take me a minute to
get the one I want. Okay with you?"

"Yes, of course." Carrie tried to sound polite as
she picked up her sweater and started folding it
again. Now that she'd established his credentials,
his presence didn't matter. She could finish packing while he made his repairs, and then get
dressed after he was through. She heard him open
the door and called after him, "Leave it ajar if it's
easier for you."

"Thanks, ma'am. I'll do that."

Carrie barely had time to start fitting her sandy
beach shoes into a plastic bag before she heard the
door open again. "Do you have much trouble with
this sort of thing?" she asked politely, not even
looking up as she heard him come in the hall behind her.

"Not really. You're the only one who ever bothered me."

The quiet words made Carrie clutch the side of
her suitcase as if she'd suddenly received an elec-
tric shock. She shut her eyes like a relative afraid

to view the remains. Delusions came with a lack of sleep, she told herself, and turned slowly around.

Mark was leaning against the bedroom wall surveying her dispassionately. If her pale cheeks and stricken expression made any impression on him, it wasn't evident in his next words. "Your manners leave a lot of room for improvement. What in the devil do you mean by hanging up on me?" he asked, moving ominously toward her. "Try it once more and you'll be damned sorry. Understand?"

Carrie's temper had been sizzling from the moment she set eyes on him. She opened her mouth to tell him in detail why he was the last man in the world she wanted to see, but when she discovered that he was even angrier, she could only stare up at him in complete confusion.

"Did you hear what I said?" he grated out. "And don't get any ideas about leaving. The door's locked, and Ben's been well paid to disappear."

"You bribed him." That seemed to be the only thing Carrie could use for an offensive tactic, and it sounded feeble even to her.

"I rewarded him for his help." Mark's glance was icy, but his stance wasn't so rigid. He was still in the same rumpled jacket and pants he'd worn on the cruiser, but Carrie could see that the effects of time and weather extended beyond his wearing apparel. His chin was unshaven and the lines of fatigue at the corners of his mouth and eyes made him look five years older. Even at that, he was far from needing pity. Anger crackled in his voice as his glance took in her suitcase on the bed. "I thought you'd try a damn fool dodge like running out. Otherwise we could have talked things over at a decent hour. Civilized people use their heads...."

"Civilized!" Carrie flared back. "You talk about being civilized after what you pulled on me yesterday? Leaving me to sit on that miserable soaking pier for hours!"

"My god, you weren't fool enough to sit around out there, I hope."

"A lot you'd have cared, even if I had. I could have died, for all the interest you showed." After the words were out, Carrie realized that they weren't the scathing, logical condemnation she'd rehearsed for hours.

Mark evidently agreed. "Oh, don't be an idiot!" he snapped, moving to stare angrily out the window.

Reason didn't come into Carrie's next action. It was pure instinct. The unwieldy plastic package of beach shoes left a lot to be desired as a weapon, but it was the first unattached thing she could see.

Her aim caught him squarely in the middle of the back. It did no injury whatsoever, but the impact was enough to make him whirl with a growl of rage. "Throw things, will you! I'll show you what happens when a woman pulls a damn fool stunt like tossing a . . ." His glance flickered down to identify the lethal weapon. As he took in the ridiculous tennis shoes in an untidy heap at his feet, his shoulders started to shake. When he finally looked up, Carrie could see that his eyes were brimming with laughter. "My god," he got out finally, "was that the best you could find?"

Carrie nodded. And then, because it simply wasn't worth the effort any longer, she went over and put her arms around his neck. "I've been so worried," she whispered into his shirt front. "I didn't know what happened to you. I thought I'd go out of my mind . . ." She broke off because she found herself caught in a grip that threatened to break every rib she owned. Mark's cheek was against the top of her head, and she could feel the bristle on his chin as he bent to nuzzle behind her ear.

"You weren't the only one," he managed. "How do you think I felt—wondering all night if you'd gotten back safely. Then, when you hung up on me this morning . . ."

". . . you were so relieved you wanted to smack me." Her fingers smoothed the back of his head with loving care. "Fine thing. And I thought you were a gentleman!"

"I've been a gentleman so long with you that I ache in every bone, and a lot of other places besides." He put her from him with an effort. "After I managed not to seduce you on the boat, I'll be damned if I'm going to break my record in a hotel room." He had her at arm's length, but his hands caressed her lightly clad figure with sure possession.

Carrie took a deep breath and drew away while

she was still able to. If Mark could make her feel like this when he'd been chasing around the Atlantic half the night, it didn't warrant thinking about what he could accomplish if he made love in earnest. She shuddered with longing and felt a warmth surge over her cheeks.

Mark apparently translated her thoughts without difficulty, and his smile made her color deepen. "I know exactly how you feel," he said softly. "I've known all along. That's one reason this has been such a hell of a week."

"Do you have time to tell me about it?"

"All the time in the world ... now." He rubbed a hand over his bristly chin. "I couldn't take a chance on your disappearing, or I'd have gone home to clean up first."

"As if that made any difference." Carrie's fierce tone told him that she would have felt the same if he'd appeared in a sheet with a full-grown beard. "Shall I phone for coffee?"

He shook his head and settled into a chair. "Then you'd never dislodge me. It's a mistake to even sit down."

Her glance was tender. "If you fall asleep, I'll just ask the maid to dust around you. She won't mind; you're a definite addition to the decor in here."

"I'll do my best to stay awake." He gestured toward her suitcase. "Keep on packing."

"As soon as I got rid of your friend Ben, I was going to get dressed."

Mark leaned back in his chair to let his masculine glance go over her. Then he shook his head. "It goes against all my instincts to agree with you. At least remember to pack the robe on top."

Carrie smiled and gathered a handful of lingerie before heading for the dressing room. "If I leave this door open, I can hear everything." A moment later, her voice floated out, "I want to know all about what happened. Don't leave anything out. . . ."

"You're a greedy little thing. Where do I start?"

Her tousled head appeared around the doorway. "When you ran out on me like a no-good heel, that's where."

"Carrie . . ." His voice was a warning. "Don't tempt me."

"All right . . . maybe you thought you were doing the proper thing . . ."

"I damn well know I was." He was emphatic. "Get some clothes on."

She wrinkled her nose but disappeared obediently. "At least you could have explained things," she called out. "I felt like a fool when that sheriff's deputy came to pick me up. Heaven knows what he thought."

A snort showed that Mark wasn't impressed. "There wasn't time to argue with you. And if I'd given you an inkling that you couldn't come along, I would have had to rope and tie you before putting you ashore."

"You're hard to satisfy," she said, darting her head out for a reproachful look. "The first time, you wouldn't let me off the miserable boat, and yesterday you couldn't wait to see the back of me."

"Carrie, be reasonable. It wasn't an Easter-egg hunt. Rudy had everything staked on this gamble, and the showdown was no place for you. I'd do exactly the same thing again."

There was a moment's silence while she thought that over. Her tone was mild when she finally said, "What happened when you took out after Rudy's cruiser?"

"I got through on the radio and arranged for surveillance. By the time the helicopter located their moorage in Skull Creek, I'd transferred to one of the patrol units. The customs chief thought I was out of my mind when I told him about your theory. So we were all relieved when the cruiser slipped out of the moorage about midnight and headed for open water to the south—this time without running lights."

Carrie appeared in the doorway, her eyes glistening with excitement. "Then how did you follow?"

"With radar and some other equipment a lot more sophisticated. We stayed well back, and fortunately the weather cooperated. With that much wind, we didn't have to worry about fog, and the rain kept them off the deck. From the way they held course, I think they felt completely safe."

"What happened then?" she breathed.

He grinned. "I came as close to getting seasick

as I care to. I'd forgotten all about taking a pill until it was too late."

"Serves you right," she told him severely. "If I'd been along, I could have reminded you."

"The boatswain would have led me to the rail. Fortunately, it wasn't necessary," Mark said dryly. "Go put your shoes on."

She bobbed out of sight again. "Well, what happened then? After you got sick, I mean?"

"I *wasn't* sick...."

"After you *felt* sick...."

"I'm sorry that I ever mentioned the subject." He heard her smothered laughter, grinned himself, and went on. "The Coast Guard let them get almost to international waters before they sounded a warning. Once they cut the siren loose, the patrol boat moved up so fast that the Down Easter looked dead in the water. Remind me not to ever try and outrun Uncle Sam."

"It'll be at the top of my list." She came out of the dressing room wearing a green wool dress and carrying her coat and a plastic cosmetics bag, which she tucked into the top of the suitcase. "Don't stop now," she said as Mark yawned and got to his feet. "What happened when you went aboard? Angela wasn't there, was she?"

"No. Just Rudy and the crewman. You were right all along the line. I'm beginning to wonder if you read tea leaves as a hobby."

"Not yet, but I'll remember if I need extra money for the grocery budget." She pretended to frown. "I wish you'd stop sidetracking me."

He looked amused. "I wouldn't even try. Incidentally, you'll probably get a letter of appreciation from the authorities."

"Oh, that . . ." She waved a deprecating hand. "I'd rather know what Rudy had in mind."

"There's not much doubt he planned to rendezvous with a small Cuban freighter as soon as he got out of our waters. The Coast Guard patrol planes had been keeping a watch on it. Fortunately, the authorities closed in fast enough that he wasn't able to get rid of the contraband. They caught him with the classified electronic parts still on board. Numbered parts that weren't included in his official inventory count. Rudy wasn't talking after his arrest, but even a lawyer like Jason Wright can't work miracles."

"Did you find the wig?"

Mark nodded, his eyes alight with laughter. "Stuffed in a sail locker. I think that was the thing that made Rudy the maddest of all."

"I'm not surprised. He'd traded on his profile and family dominance so long that he was convinced he was invulnerable. Think what it did to his ego when you saw through his disguise and caught him hiding in Angela's clothes."

"I don't know about the psychological hangups, but the air was scorched and blue when a customs man waved that long-haired wig around for everybody to see."

"Do you suppose that Rudy took the electronic parts aboard yesterday?"

"Probably. They didn't require much room, but

Rudy couldn't have taken a chance in stowing them on the boat much earlier. I imagine they were carried on in the boxes and baskets for 'Angela's' party aboard. And we would have followed right along with his planning if you hadn't overheard his sister with Jason Wright in Savannah."

Carrie smiled as she started to close her suitcase. "I'm glad that something good came of it . . . besides my friend the hippo."

"You mean that ridiculous creature you left aboard?"

She looked up, and her smile deepened. "He grows on you. I thought your niece might like him in her menagerie."

"She undoubtedly will. I'll let you present it in person after we're married." Mark moved forward to lift her suitcase. "Ready to go?"

Carrie stood motionless with her arm in one coat sleeve. "What did you say?"

"I asked if you were ready to go."

"Before that. . . ."

"I just said you could take the hippo along when we meet my sister and her family." He looked at his watch. "Roberta's arranging the wedding today at her church in Savannah and plans to be your matron of honor. I told her we'd arrive about noon."

"You can't be serious. . . ."

"Never more so." He took her bag out into the hallway and then came back to briskly help her on with her coat. "And if you have any thoughts of resistance—give up. You haven't a chance. Everybody on that patrol boat last night knew what had happened between us, and they're all on my side. If you'd tried to run out on me this morning, you wouldn't have gotten far."

Carrie wondered whether her light-headedness came from a lack of sleep or the pounding of her heart. "You're crazy," she managed to say. "I haven't done anything wrong."

"I didn't say you had. The sheriff's patrol would just have brought you politely back to the inn while they checked to see if your license was in order."

She stared at him. "And I suppose the next thing would have been an audit on my income tax."

He considered that carefully. "I forgot about *that* one."

"It's just as well. How did the Coast Guard figure in it? Unless I'd decided to swim to the mainland."

"I can't remember right now, but . . ."

". . . you'd have thought of something."

"You'd better believe it." He started to smile. "Persistence is my middle name. You can ask Rudy for a testimonial."

Carrie suspected that Mark was enjoying their exchange just as much as she was. But underlying his amusement was a current of steady determination that made her breath catch in her throat.

"Honestly, Mark, you can't just walk in here and start ordering me around," she said, trying to sound brisk.

"It worked once. I don't see why it won't again." He came a little closer. "Relax, my love. You aren't convincing anybody." His eyes suddenly narrowed with laughter. "I remember now where the Coast Guard comes in. The commander is a buddy of the federal judge in Savannah who's supplying the marriage license."

Carrie put up a hand to make him keep his distance. "You're going too fast, I tell you."

"Why? Did I forget something?"

"Yes." She swallowed. "An honest proposal."

The firm lines of his mouth softened. "All right. How about 'I love you, Carrie'? I love every last thing about you. This past week has shown me that I can't do without you, and I knew ten minutes after we met that I wanted to make love to you." His eyes darkened. "I still do, and it's a hell of an effort to postpone it."

Carrie's heartbeat sounded like thunder in her ears as she smiled tremulously up at him. "Just so long as we don't honeymoon alongside that shrimp-boat dock."

He threw back his head and laughed. "Don't worry. I think you deserve a little better. Maybe four walls and a floor that doesn't move up and down all the time. Otherwise, it doesn't matter to me. Just so you're there."

She had trouble getting her voice under control to tease him. "After these last two nights, you must be so tired that you could sleep standing up in a phone booth. . . ."

"Possibly. After three nights without sleep, I'll let you know," he told her.

"Darling . . . be sensible," she begged. "Maybe we should wait a day or so."

Her halfhearted protest brought an entirely different expression to his face. He bent down suddenly, hauled her into his arms, and covered her parted lips. At first, his mouth was gentle and softly searching, until he felt her response. Then the kiss hardened with urgency and desire surfacing in a storm that made Carrie's body melt against his hard masculine strength. When Mark finally raised his head, she had to cling to his shoulders to keep from falling.

"Still want to be sensible?" he asked in a voice that wasn't as steady as he imagined.

Carrie shook her head emphatically. She might be unable to breathe, and a strange sweet languor had taken possession of her, but she knew the answer to his question. "You have me so confused by now, I don't even know what the word 'sensible' means," she admitted. Then, as he started to chuckle, she added casually, "Besides, I forgot that you won't have to be up early in the morning. You'll get some rest after all."

Mark's eyebrows rose in appreciation. "Trust a woman to get to the heart of the matter," he said, moving her firmly toward the door. "Three nights without sleep obviously calls for three days in bed to compensate. Now, why didn't I think of that?"

"Perhaps you had other things on your mind. It was easier for me."

"What do you mean?"

"I could think of only one thing—that I love you, love you, love you." Once she'd said it, she didn't want to stop.

Mark's glance embraced her with slow possessiveness. "This day and forever more?"

"This day and forever more," she said with conviction.

"That, my sweetest Carrie," he told her softly, "is all I'll ever want to hear."

About the Author

Glenna Finley is a native of Washington State. She earned her degree from Stanford University in Russian Studies and in Speech and Dramatic Arts, with emphasis on radio.

After a stint in radio and publicity work in Seattle, she went to New York City to work for NBC as a producer in its international division. In addition, she worked with the "March of Time" and *Life* magazine.

As a producer, she had her own show about activities in Manhattan, a show that was broadcast to England. The programs were similar to those of the "Voice of America."

Though her life in New York was exciting, she eventually returned to the Northwest where she married. Currently residing in Seattle with her husband, Donald Witte, and their son, she loves to travel, and draws heavily on her travels and experiences for the novels that have been published. Her books for NAL have sold several million copies.

Big Bestsellers from SIGNET

☐ **THE KILLING GIFT** by Bari Wood.
(#E7350—$2.25)

☐ **WHITE FIRES BURNING** by Catherine Dillon.
(#E7351—$1.75)

☐ **CONSTANTINE CAY** by Catherine Dillon.
(#W6892—$1.50)

☐ **THE SECRET LIST OF HEINRICH ROEHM** by Michael
Barak.
(#E7352—$1.75)

☐ **YESTERDAY'S CHILD** by Helene Brown.
(#E7353—$1.75)

☐ **FOREVER AMBER** by Kathleen Winsor.
(#J7360—$1.95)

☐ **SMOULDERING FIRES** by Anya Seton.
(#J7276—$1.95)

☐ **HARVEST OF DESIRE** by Rochelle Larkin.
(#J7277—$1.95)

☐ **THE HOUSE ON THE LEFT BANK** by Velda Johnston.
(#W7279—$1.50)

☐ **A ROOM WITH DARK MIRRORS** by Velda Johnston.
(#W7143—$1.50)

☐ **THE PERSIAN PRICE** by Evelyn Anthony.
(#J7254—$1.95)

☐ **EARTHSOUND** by Arthur Herzog.   (#E7255—$1.75)

☐ **THE DEVIL'S OWN** by Christopher Nicole.
(#J7256—$1.95)

☐ **THE GREEK TREASURE** by Irving Stone.
(#E7211—$2.25)

☐ **THE GATES OF HELL** by Harrison Salisbury.
(#E7213—$2.25)

THE NEW AMERICAN LIBRARY, INC.,
P.O. Box 999, Bergenfield, New Jersey 07621

Please send me the SIGNET BOOKS I have checked above. I am
enclosing $_____(check or money order—no currency
or C.O.D.'s). Please include the list price plus 35¢ a copy to cover
handling and mailing costs. (Prices and numbers are subject to
change without notice.)

Name_____

Address_____

City_____State_____Zip Code_____
Allow at least 4 weeks for delivery

More Big Bestsellers from SIGNET

- [ ] **SAVAGE EDEN** by Constance Gluyas. (#J7171—$1.95)
- [ ] **ROSE: MY LIFE IN SERVICE** by Rosina Harrison.
  (#J7174—$1.95)
- [ ] **THE FINAL FIRE** by Dennis Smith. (#J7141—$1.95)
- [ ] **SOME KIND OF HERO** by James Kirkwood.
  (#J7142—$1.95)
- [ ] **THE SAMURAI** by George Macbeth. (#J7021—$1.95)
- [ ] **THE HOMOSEXUAL MATRIX** by C. A. Tripp.
  (#E7172—$2.50)
- [ ] **CBS: Reflections in a Bloodshot Eye** by Robert Metz.
  (#E7115—$2.25)
- [ ] **'SALEM'S LOT** by Stephen King. (#J7112—$1.95)
- [ ] **CARRIE** by Stephen King. (#E6410—$1.75)
- [ ] **FATU-HIVA: Back to Nature** by Thor Heyerdahl.
  (#J7113—$1.95)
- [ ] **THE DOMINO PRINCIPLE** by Adam Kennedy.
  (#J7058—$1.95)
- [ ] **IF YOU COULD SEE WHAT I HEAR** by Tom Sullivan and Derek Gill. (#W7061—$1.50)
- [ ] **THE PRACTICE OF PLEASURE** by Michael Harris.
  (#E7059—$1.75)
- [ ] **ENGAGEMENT** by Eloise Weld. (#E7060—$1.75)
- [ ] **FOR THE DEFENSE** by F. Lee Bailey. (#J7022—$1.95)

THE NEW AMERICAN LIBRARY, INC.,
P.O. Box 999, Bergenfield, New Jersey 07621

Please send me the SIGNET BOOKS I have checked above. I am enclosing $_____(check or money order—no currency or C.O.D.'s). Please include the list price plus 35¢ a copy to cover handling and mailing costs. (Prices and numbers are subject to change without notice.)

Name_____

Address_____

City_____State_____Zip Code_____
Allow at least 4 weeks for delivery

FREE BOOK OFFER!

New American Library wants to bring you the type of books you enjoy. For this reason we are asking you to fill out our questionnaire so that we can learn more about your reading tastes. For your effort we will send you a FREE copy of THE NEW AMERICAN WEBSTER HANDY COLLEGE DICTIONARY.

1. Are you_____female_____male?

2. What is your age?
_____ Under 15
_____ 15 to 24
_____ 25 to 34
_____ 35 to 44
_____ 45 to 54
_____ 55 or over

3. What is your level of education?
_____ Currently   Jr. High_____H.S._____College_____
_____ Some High School
_____ High School Graduate
_____ Some College
_____ College Graduate

4. What is your income level?
_____ Under $10,000
_____ $10,000 to $14,999
_____ $15,000 to $19,999
_____ $20,000 to $24,999
_____ $25,000 and up

5. Where did you buy this book?
_____ Bookstore
_____ Drugstore
_____ Chain Variety Store
_____ Supermarket
_____ Department Store
_____ Discount Store
_____ Newsstand
_____ Bus or Train Station
_____ Airport
_____ Other

(Please Specify)

Please turn page

6. **How many paperback books have you bought in the last six months?**
_____ 1 to 3
_____ 4 to 6
_____ 7 to 9
_____ 10 or more

7. **What types of books do you like best?**
_____ Hardcover bestsellers when available in paperback
_____ Romantic Novels
_____ Historical Novels
_____ Mystery and Suspense Thrillers
_____ Science Fiction
_____ Cookbooks
_____ Self Help and How-To Books
_____ Biography and Autobiography
_____ Other_____

8. **Why did you buy this book?**_____
(You may check more than one answer)   *Give title*
_____ Recognized the title
_____ Author's reputation
_____ The book's cover
_____ Price
_____ Friend's recommendation
_____ Newspaper or magazine ad
_____ Radio ad
_____ TV ad
_____ Store display
_____ Saw author on TV, or heard him on radio
_____ Book review
_____ Free instore booklet
_____ Subject matter
_____ Other_____
           (Please Specify)

If you do not wish to include your name and address, please do indicate the name of your town and state.

Please return your questionnaire and coupon to:

— —

New American Library, 120 Woodbine St., Bergenfield, New Jersey 07621

Please send me a free copy of THE NEW AMERICAN WEBSTER HANDY COLLEGE DICTIONARY (#Q7252).

NAME_____

ADDRESS_____

CITY_____STATE_____ZIP_____

THIS OFFER EXPIRES JUNE 30, 1977